U0561771

孔子学院总部/国家汉办推荐
Recommended by Confucius Institute Headquarters (Hanban)

TANG POETRY IN PAINTINGS

畫說唐詩

许渊冲◎译

陈佩秋 等◎绘

中国出版集团

中译出版社

目录 CONTENTS

VI 唐诗步入百姓家
Tang Poetry: Appealing to All

I

V

唐诗步入百姓家

唐朝为中国古典诗歌的全盛时期，名家辈出，流派纷呈，诗歌艺术气象万千。李白、杜甫、白居易、王维、李商隐等诗人作品成就了唐诗艺术的高峰，千余年来影响深远。

《唐诗三百首》成书于清乾隆二十八年（1763），系孙洙所辑。全书选录了七十余位诗人三百一十首唐诗。

孙洙字临西（一作芩西），号蘅塘，晚号退士，无锡人。生于康熙辛卯（1711）七月初十，卒于乾隆戊戌（1778）十二月初七，享年六十八，葬景云乡陈湾里。乾隆十六年（1751）进士，曾任山东邹平县令，江宁府教授，著有《蘅塘漫稿》。史载孙洙"性颖敏，家贫"，为官清廉，问民疾苦，与民讲学，民感其仁。其终身不改书生本色，老而勤学。

自《唐诗三百首》问世以来，各种刊印本、注释本层出不穷，两百多年来风行海内外，几至家置一编。《唐诗三百首》初衷面向塾学子弟，乃童蒙读本，但因所选唐诗兼顾不同时期诗风特点和诗人流派风格，范围广泛，便于吟诵，精到浅显且具代表性，深受读者喜爱，终成雅俗共赏的一部传统读物。

余幼时恰逢十年浩劫，未能一睹《唐诗三百首》。待云开日出喜获《唐诗三百首》之时，已过启蒙岁月，只能聊作零星吟咏而已。然对《唐诗三百首》的偏爱时至今日依旧，不经意间搜罗的各种版本已有十数种。曾读过坊间刊有配图的《唐诗三百首》，或刻工粗俗或构图简陋，皆未能表达出唐诗之真实意境，实为一大憾事。

乙酉（2005）岁末，余曾酝酿以孙洙的《唐诗三百首》为蓝本，遍邀海上画师配画，后因诸多因素搁浅。庚寅（2010）伊始，方案重新启动。历时两年，有幸得到陈佩秋、林曦明、陈家泠、戴敦邦、张桂铭、韩天衡、杨正新、萧海春、韩硕、张培成、卢甫圣、施大畏、车鹏飞、朱新昌、马小娟、朱敏、丁小方和何曦共十八位当今海上丹青高手鼎力相助。最终以一百零八首唐诗绘就一百零八幅作品，皆为一时精心之作，可谓是当代海派绘画艺术的一次盛会。后又承蒙陈佩秋先生和高式熊先生两位前辈厚爱，分别题写和篆刻了"画说唐诗"，为此佳话画上了一个圆满的句号。

今上海清河文化传播有限公司与孔子学院总部、中译出版社合作推出中英文对照的《画说唐诗》，将有助于世界各国人民对中国传统文化的理解，增进中国人民与世界各国人民的友谊。《画说唐诗》与唐诗英文翻译家许渊冲教授的牵手是一种缘分，希冀英汉对照、一诗一画的《画说唐诗》可以飞得更高，走得更远。

费滨海

壬辰大暑于谷庵

Tang Poetry: Appealing to All

The Tang Dynasty was the heyday of classical Chinese poetry. A good many outstanding poets of various schools brought prosperity to the art of poetry. Among them, Li Bai, Du Fu, Bai Juyi, Wang Wei and Li Shangyin contributed the most to the boom of Tang poetry. Their works have produced a far-reaching influence over the past one thousand years.

The *Three Hundred Tang Poems* was compiled by Sun Zhu in 1763, the 28th year of Emperor Qianlong's reign in the Qing Dynasty. The whole book includes 310 poems composed by over 70 poets.

A native of Wuxi, Sun Zhu was also known as Linxi or Qinxi (courtesy name) and Hengtang or Tuishi (literary name). He was born on July 10 (Chinese lunar calendar) in 1711, the 50th year of Emperor Kangxi's reign in the Qing Dynasty, and passed away at the age of 68 on December 7 (Chinese lunar calendar) in 1778, the 43rd year of Emperor Qianlong's reign, buried at Chenwanli, Jingyun Village, Wuxi City. He passed the palace examination in 1751, the 16th year of Emperor Qianlong's reign, and the positions he held in the government were Magistrate of Zouping County, and Educational Official of Jiangning City, Shandong Province. His works were included in *Hengtang Causerie*. According to historical records, Sun Zhu was 'a clever and diligent man from a poor family'.

An incorruptible official, he was concerned about common people's sufferings and often gave lectures to them, which touched them deeply. He was always a diligent learner in his lifetime, even in his later years.

Since it came out over two centuries ago, *Three Hundred Tang Poems* has been very popular at home and abroad with numerous editions in different prints and annotations. At the prime time, almost every Chinese household kept one copy of the book. Although designed to be a primer for students of traditional Chinese private schools, the book has turned out to cater to both refined and popular tastes. All easy to recite, the selected poems cover different styles and subjects and represent the best works of poets of different schools and in different periods.

I did not have the chance to read *Three Hundred Tang Poems* when I was a child because of the Cultural Revolution. When I eventually got the book, it was not my best age to read it any more so I only recited some of the poems occasionally. However, I have enjoyed reading it since then and collected dozens of versions of this book. I have also come across some inferior versions with rough illustrations and coarse printings. None of them helped to display the real charm of Tang poems. It is a pity for such a classic!

At the end of 2005, I planned to invite painters of the Shanghai School to illustrate Sun Zhu's version of the book. But the plan was shelved for various reasons until early 2010. Over the past two years, each of the 108 Tang poems has been illustrated with a delicate painting thanks to the support of 18 outstanding painters of the Shanghai School, including Chen Peiqiu, Lin Ximing, Chen Jialing, Dai Dunbang, Zhang Guiming, Han Tianheng, Yang Zhengxin, Xiao Haichun, Han Shuo, Zhang Peicheng, Lu Fusheng, Shi Dawei, Che Pengfei, Zhu Xinchang, Ma Xiaojuan, Zhu Min, Ding Xiaofang and He Xi. It is like a selected collection of contemporary Shanghai School paintings. Moreover, Mr. Chen Peiqiu and Mr. Gao Shixiong respectively inscribed and engraved the four Chinese characters 'Hua Shuo Tang Shi' (Tang Poetry in Paintings) for the new book, drawing the collective effort to a successful conclusion.

The Chinese-English *Tang Poetry in Paintings* is jointly published by Shanghai Qinghe Culture and Communication Co., Ltd., Confucius Institute Headquarters, and China Translation and Publishing House. It is intended to help the world better understand traditional Chinese culture and cement the friendship between China and the world. The participation of Mr. Xu Yuanchong, a senior expert in translating Tang poetry into English, only adds luster to the book. Lastly, I would like to wish the book a great success both at home and abroad.

Fei Binhai

Written in Gu'an Hut on July 22, 2012

秋日登吴公台上寺远眺

刘长卿

古台摇落后，
秋入望乡心。
野寺来人少，
云峰隔水深。
夕阳依旧垒，
寒磬满空林。
惆怅南朝事，
长江独至今。

Gazing Afar from a Southern Temple on an Autumn Day

Liu Changqing

The ancient temple strewn with fallen leaves,

Autumn invades a homesick heart and grieves.

Unvisited monasteries wild would seem

With cloudy peaks beyond deep stream on stream.

The setting sun sinks behind mountains high;

The chill bell fills the dale with sigh on sigh.

Brooding over Southern Dynasties' fall,

The lonely Rivers flows in spite of all.

感 遇（其四）

张九龄

江南有丹橘，
经冬犹绿林。
岂伊地气暖，
自有岁寒心。
可以荐嘉客，
奈何阻重深。
运命惟所遇，
循环不可寻。
徒言树桃李，
此木岂无阴？

感遇（其四） 陈家泠 绘

The Oranges Painter: Chen Jialing

The Oranges

Zhang Jiuling

South of the river grows the orange tree,

Its leaves are green throughout the winter long.

From snow and frost is its warmer soil free?

By nature its fruit is cold-proof and strong.

It is worthy to entertain your guest,

But distance keeps it far away from you.

By fate the east stands far apart from the west,

Oh, how can the old again become new?

You may plant as you like peach or plum trees,

But orange trees may afford shade to please.

月下独酌　韩硕 绘
Drinking Alone under the Moon　Painter: Han Shuo

月下独酌

李白

花间一壶酒，
独酌无相亲。
举杯邀明月，
对影成三人。
月既不解饮，
影徒随我身。
暂伴月将影，
行乐须及春。
我歌月徘徊，
我舞影零乱。
醒时同交欢，
醉后各分散。
永结无情游，
相期邈云汉。

Drinking Alone under the Moon

Li Bai

Among the flowers, from a pot of wine

I drink without a companion of mine.

I raise my cup to invite the Moon who blends

Her light with my Shadow and we're three friends.

The Moon does not know how to drink her share;

In vain my Shadow follows me here and there.

Together with them for the time I stay,

And make merry before spring's spent away.

I sing and the Moon lingers to hear my song;

My Shadow's a mess while I dance along.

Sober, we three remain cheerful and gay;

Drunken, we part and each may go his way.

Our friendship will outshine all earthly love;

Next time we'll meet beyond the stars above.

春 思

李白

燕草如碧丝，
秦桑低绿枝。
当君怀归日，
是妾断肠时。
春风不相识，
何事入罗帏？

春思　朱新昌 绘

A Faithful Wife Longing for Her Husband in Spring　Painter: Zhu Xinchang

A Faithful Wife Longing for Her Husband in Spring

Li Bai

Northern grass looks like green silk thread;

Western mulberries bend their head.

When you think of your home on your part,

Already broken is my heart.

Vernal wind, intruder unseen,

O how dare you part my bed screen!

望岳 卢甫圣 绘 ▶

Gazing on Mount Tai Painter: Lu Fusheng

望 岳

杜甫

岱宗夫如何？
齐鲁青未了。
造化钟神秀，
阴阳割昏晓。
荡胸生层云，
决眦入归鸟。
会当凌绝顶，
一览众山小。

Gazing on Mount Tai

Du Fu

O peak of peaks, how high it stands!

One boundless green overspreads two States.

A marvel done by Nature's hands,

Over light and shade it dominates.

Clouds rise therefrom and lave my breast;

I stretch my eyes to see birds fleet.

I will ascend the mountain's crest;

It dwarfs all peaks under my feet.

昔別君未婚
兒女忽成行
明日隔山岳
世事兩茫茫
杜甫

贈衛八處士
辛卯年初夏
范曾

赠卫八处士

杜甫

人生不相见，动如参与商。
今夕复何夕，共此灯烛光。
少壮能几时，鬓发各已苍。
访旧半为鬼，惊呼热中肠。
焉知二十载，重上君子堂。
昔别君未婚，儿女忽成行。
怡然敬父执，问我来何方。
问答乃未已，驱儿罗酒浆。
夜雨剪春韭，新炊间黄粱。
主称会面难，一举累十觞。
十觞亦不醉，感子故意长。
明日隔山岳，世事两茫茫。

赠卫八处士　戴敦邦 绘
For Wei the Eighth　Painter: Dai Dunbang

For Wei the Eighth

Du Fu

How rarely together friends are!
As Morning Star with Evening Star.
O what a fair night is tonight!
Together we share candlelight.
How long can last our youthful years?
Gray hair on our temples appears.
We find half of our friends departed.
How can we not cry broken-hearted!
After twenty years, who knows then
I come into your hall again?
Unmarried twenty years ago,
Now you have children in a row.
Seeing their father's friend at home,
They're glad to ask where I come from.
Our talk has not come to an end,
When wine is offered to a friend.
They bring leeks cut after night rain
And millet cooked with new grain.
The host says, 'It is hard to meet.
Let us drink ten cups of wine sweet!'
Ten cupfuls cannot make me drunk,
For deep in your love I am sunk.
Mountains will divide us tomorrow,
O what can we foresee but sorrow!

佳人 朱新昌 绘

A Lovely Woman Painter: Zhu Xinchang

佳 人

（选段）

杜 甫

绝代有佳人，
幽居在空谷。
自云良家子，
零落依草木。
……
摘花不插发，
采柏动盈掬。
天寒翠袖薄，
日暮倚修竹。

A Lovely Woman

(Selected Verse)

Du Fu

A lovely woman of her days,

In a secluded vale she stays.

Brought up in a good family,

She lives amid wild greenery.

She wears no flower in her hair,

But picks pine-seed with hands so fair.

Shivering in her thin sleeves green,

At sunset on bamboos she'll lean.

送綦毋潜落第还乡

（选段）

王维

置酒长安道，
同心与我违。
行当浮桂棹，
未几拂荆扉。
远树带行客，
孤城当落晖。
吾谋适不用，
勿谓知音稀。

送綦毋潜落第还乡　丁小方 绘

Seeing Qiwu Qian Off after His Failure in Civil Service Examinations *Painter: Ding Xiaofang*

画说唐诗

Seeing Qiwu Qian Off after His Failure in Civil Service Examinations

(Selected Verse)

Wang Wei

We drink adieu on the broad way,

My bosom friend's going away.

Your orchid boat will sail before,

Until you reach your cottage door.

Far-off trees show the roaming one,

A lonely town in setting sun.

Though you have not achieved your end,

Do not belie your bosom friend!

青 溪

王 维

言入黄花川，
每逐青溪水。
随山将万转，
趣途无百里。
声喧乱石中，
色静深松里。
漾漾泛菱荇，
澄澄映葭苇。
我心素已闲，
清川澹如此。
请留盘石上，
垂钓将已矣。

The Blue Stream

Wang Wei

I follow the Blue Rill

To the Stream of Yellow Blooms.

It winds from hill to hill

Till far away it looms.

It roars amid pebbles white

And calms down under pines green.

Weeds float on ripples light,

Reeds mirrored like a screen.

Mind's carefree, alone;

The clear stream flows with ease.

I would sit on a stone

To fish whatever I please.

斜陽照墟落 窮巷牛羊歸 即此羨閒逸 悵然吟式微

王維渭川田家詩意圖 戴敦邦北京寓

渭川田家

王 维

斜阳照墟落，
穷巷牛羊归。
野老念牧童，
倚杖候荆扉。
雉雊麦苗秀，
蚕眠桑叶稀。
田夫荷锄至，
相见语依依。
即此羡闲逸，
怅然吟式微。

渭川田家 戴敦邦 绘
Rural Scene by River Wei Painter: Dai Dunbang

Rural Scene by River Wei

Wang Wei

The village lit by slanting rays,

The cattle trail on homeward ways.

See an old man for the herd wait,

Leaning on staff by wicket gate.

Pheasants call in wheat field with ease,

Silkworms sleep on sparse mulberries.

Shouldering hoe, two ploughmen meet;

They talk long, standing on their feet.

For this unhurried life I long,

Lost in singing 'Home-going song'.

西施咏　朱新昌 绘 ▶

Song of the Beauty of the West Painter: Zhu Xinchang

西施咏

王维

艳色天下重，
西施宁久微。
朝为越溪女，
暮作吴宫妃。
贱日岂殊众，
贵来方悟稀。
邀人傅脂粉，
不自著罗衣。
君宠益娇态，
君怜无是非。
当时浣纱伴，
莫得同车归。
持谢邻家子，
效颦安可希。

Song of the Beauty of the West

Wang Wei

A beauty is loved far and wide.

How could she be unknown for long?

At dawn she washed by riverside;

At dusk to the king she'd belong.

Poor, she was one of lower race;

Ennobled, she's one of the few.

She has maids to powder her face

And dress her up with silk robe new.

Royal favor adds to her charms;

Royal love turns wrong into right.

Her companions wash with bare arms.

Could they attain such royal height?

To washerwomen I should say:

Don't follow her unusual way!

夏日南亭怀辛大

孟浩然

山光忽西落，
池月渐东上。
散发乘夕凉，
开轩卧闲敞。
荷风送香气，
竹露滴清响。
欲取鸣琴弹，
恨无知音赏。
感此怀故人，
终宵劳梦想。

夏日南亭怀辛大　卢甫圣 绘

Thinking of Xin the Eldest by the Poolside on a Summer Day Painter: Lu Fusheng

Thinking of Xin the Eldest by the Poolside on a Summer Day

Meng Haoran

Suddenly sunlight fades o'er Western Hill;

Gradually moonbeams spread on Eastern Pool.

With hair uncombed, I lie in evening still;

With windows opened, I enjoy the cool.

The lotus spreads its fragrance in the breeze;

Dew drips on the bamboo with a sound clear.

I would play on my lute a tune to please,

But where can I find a connoisseur's ear?

I think of you, my dear friend out of sight,

But you come into my dream at midnight.

宿业师山房待丁大不至　丁小方 绘

Waitinging in Vain for Ding the Eldest Painter: Ding Xiaofang

宿业师山房待丁大不至

孟浩然

夕阳度西岭，
群壑倏已暝。
松月生夜凉，
风泉满清听。
樵人归欲尽，
烟鸟栖初定。
之子期宿来，
孤琴候萝径。

Waitinging in Vain for Ding the Eldest

Meng Haoran

The western ridge with setting sun is crowned.

And all the dales in the gloaming are drowned.

The moon sheds chilly beams on the pine trees;

The fountain's song is spread out in the breeze.

All the woodcutters come back for a rest;

All the birds go through the mist for their nest.

Waiting for Ding my dear friend all the day,

I play my lute and gaze on ivy way.

寻西山隐者不遇

（选段）

丘为

绝顶一茅茨，
直上三十里。
叩关无僮仆，
窥室惟案几。
……
草色新雨中，
松声晚窗里。
及兹契幽绝，
自足荡心耳。
……

寻西山隐者不遇　车鹏飞　绘

A Mountaintop Cottage Painter: Che Pengfei

A Mountaintop Cottage

(Selected Verse)

Qiu Wei

Your mountaintop cottage stands high,

Three thousand feet under the sky.

I knock but none answers my call;

I see but tables in the hall.

Grass grows more green after the rain;

The windows hear the pines' refrain.

In solitude I have my will.

Content, let me enjoy my fill!

宿王昌龄隐居 朱敏 绘

A Poet's Hermitage Painter: Zhu Min

宿王昌龄隐居

常建

清溪深不测，
隐处惟孤云。
松际露微月，
清光犹为君。
茅亭宿花影，
药院滋苔纹。
余亦谢时去，
西山鸾鹤群。

A Poet's Hermitage

Chang Jian

The creek so clear seems deep,

A lonely cloud in view.

Through pines the moon would peep,

And shed clear beams for you.

The flowers' shadows sleep

Under your thatched roof new.

Cranes' company I'd keep,

To moss I bid adieu.

长安遇冯著

韦应物

客从东方来，
衣上灞陵雨。
问客何为来？
采山因买斧。
冥冥花正开，
飏飏燕新乳。
昨别今已春，
鬓丝生几缕？

长安遇冯著 张培成 绘

Meeting Feng Zhu in the Capital Painter: Zhang Peicheng

Meeting Feng Zhu in the Capital

Wei Yingwu

From the east comes my friend,

Whose gown is wet with rain,

I ask him what's his end,

He would clear off the stain.

Mute, mute blow all the flowers;

Fleet, fleet new swallows play.

Spring comes after parting hours.

How much hair has turned gray?

夕次盱眙县 张培成 绘

Moored at the Pier of Xuyi Painter: Zhang Peicheng

夕次盱眙县

韦应物

落帆逗淮镇,
停舫临孤驿。
浩浩风起波,
冥冥日沉夕。
人归山郭暗,
雁下芦洲白。
独夜忆秦关,
听钟未眠客。

Moored at the Pier of Xuyi

Wei Yingwu

Lowering my sail on River Huai,

I moor my boat at lonely pier.

The wind raises wave on wave nigh;

The drear sun sinks in the west drear.

People go back to dark hillside;

On white reed bed wild geese alight.

Lonely, I lie with eyes open wide,

Sleepless, I hear the bell all night.

东 郊

韦应物

吏舍跼终年，
出郊旷清曙。
杨柳散和风，
青山澹吾虑。
依丛适自憩，
缘涧还复去。
微雨霭芳原，
春鸠鸣何处。
乐幽心屡止，
遵事迹犹遽。
终罢斯结庐，
慕陶直可庶。

东郊 韩天衡 绘
The Eastern Countryside Painter: Han Tianheng

The Eastern Countryside

Wei Yingwu

Staying in office all the year,

I go to countryside one morning clear.

Willows swing and sway in soft breeze;

Fading blue hills put my mind at ease.

I go among trees for a rest,

And along a creek east and west.

The drizzle sweetens grassy plain,

Where I hear turtledoves' refrain.

The solitude delights my heart.

How can I leave it far apart?

I would build here my hermitage

And live a life like ancient sage.

送杨氏女 戴敦邦·绘

Farewell to Miss Yang Painter: Dai Dunbang

送杨氏女

（选段）

韦应物

永日方戚戚，
出行复悠悠。
女子今有行，
大江溯轻舟。
尔辈苦无恃，
抚念益慈柔。
幼为长所育，
两别泣不休。
……

Farewell to Miss Yang

(Selected Verse)

Wei Yingwu

Oh, melancholy all the day,

Now you are going far away.

Miss Yang, you will take a light boat,

On the great River you will float.

You have no mother on whom to depend,

A helping hand to you I'll lend.

The elders have a loving heart:

Tears stream from our eyes when we part.

溪 居

柳宗元

久为簪组束，
幸此南夷谪。
闲依农圃邻，
偶似山林客。
晓耕翻露草，
夜榜响溪石。
来往不逢人，
长歌楚天碧。

溪居　车鹏飞 绘

Living by the Brookside Painter: Che Pengfei

Living by the Brookside

Liu Zongyuan

Tired of officialdom for long,

I'm glad to be banished southwest.

At leisure I hear farmer's song;

Haply I look like hillside guest.

At dawn I cut grass wet with dew;

My boat comes o'er pebbles at night.

To and fro there's no man in view;

I chant till southern sky turns bright.

塞上曲 张培成 绘

Song of the Frontier Painter: Zhang Peicheng

塞上曲

王昌龄

蝉鸣空桑林，
八月萧关道。
出塞入塞寒，
处处黄芦草。
从来幽并客，
皆共尘沙老。
莫学游侠儿，
矜夸紫骝好。

Song of the Frontier (Ⅰ)

Wang Changling

Amid the mulberries cicadas trill

In the eighth moon on the desolate frontier.

The warriors go out of the Great Wall chill,

On yellow reed overgrown there and here.

Since olden days all northern cavaliers

Have grown old on the field under war cloud.

Don't imitate your chivalric compeers,

Who only of their battle steed are proud.

塞下曲

王昌龄

饮马度秋水，
水寒风似刀。
平沙日未没，
黯黯见临洮。
昔日长城战，
咸言意气高。
黄尘足今古，
白骨乱蓬蒿。

塞下曲 张培成 绘
Song of the Frontier Painter: Zhang Peicheng

Song of the Frontier (Ⅱ)

Wang Changling

We water horses and cross autumn streams,

Like a sword on water blows the wind cold.

On sandy plain the sun sheds parting beams,

In the gloom looms the city wall of old.

By the Great Wall we fought wars in the land;

Our warriors' fighting spirit was at its height.

History is buried in the yellow sand;

Among the weeds are scattered the bones white.

子夜吴歌·秋歌 张培成 绘
Southern Ballad of Autumn Painter: Zhang Peicheng

長安一片月

萬戶搗衣聲

培成

子夜吴歌·秋歌

李白

长安一片月，
万户捣衣声。
秋风吹不尽，
总是玉关情。
何日平胡虏，
良人罢远征。

Southern Ballad of Autumn

Li Bai

Moonlight is spread over the capital,

The sound of pounding clothes far and near

Is brought by autumn wind which can't blow all

The longings away for far-off frontier.

When can we vanquish the barbarian foe

So that our men no longer into battle go?

长干行

李白

妾发初覆额，折花门前剧。
郎骑竹马来，绕床弄青梅。
同居长干里，两小无嫌猜。
十四为君妇，羞颜未尝开。
低头向暗壁，千唤不一回。
十五始展眉，愿同尘与灰。
常存抱柱信，岂上望夫台。
十六君远行，瞿塘滟滪堆。
五月不可触，猿声天上哀。
门前迟行迹，一一生绿苔。
苔深不能扫，落叶秋风早。
八月蝴蝶黄，双飞西园草。
感此伤妾心，坐愁红颜老。
早晚下三巴，预将书报家。
相迎不道远，直至长风沙。

长干行 戴敦邦 绘
Ballad of a Trader's Wife Painter: Dai Dunbang

Ballad of a Trader's Wife

Li Bai

My forehead barely covered by my hair,
Outdoors I plucked and played with flowers fair.
On hobby horse he came upon the scene;
Around the well we played with mumes still green.
We lived close neighbors on Riverside Lane,
Carefree and innocent, we children twain.
At fourteen years old I became his bride;
I often turned my bashful face aside.
Hanging my head, I'd look on the dark wall;
I would not answer his call upon call.
I was fifteen when I composed my brows;
To mix my dust with his were my dear vows.
Rather than break faith, he declared he'd die.
Who knew I'd live alone in tower high?
I was sixteen when he went far away,
Passing Three Gorges studded with rocks grey,
Where ships were wrecked when spring flood ran high,
Where gibbons' wails seemed coming from the sky.
Green moss now overgrows before our door;
His footprints, hidden, can be seen no more.
Moss can't be swept away, so thick it grows,
And leaves fall early when the west wind blows.
In yellow autumn butterflies would pass
Two by two in west garden over the grass.
The sight would break my heart and I'm afraid,
Sitting alone, my rosy cheeks would fade.
'O when are you to leave the western land?
Do not forget to tell me beforehand!
I'll walk to meet you and would not call it far
Even to go to Long Wind Beach where you are.'

游子吟 张培成 绘

Song of the Parting Son Painter: Zhang Peicheng

游子吟

孟郊

慈母手中线，
游子身上衣。
临行密密缝，
意恐迟迟归。
谁言寸草心，
报得三春晖。

Song of the Parting Son

Meng Jiao

From the threads a mother's hand weaves,

A gown for parting son is made.

Sown stitch by stitch before he leaves,

For fear his return be delayed.

Such kindness as young grass receives

From the warm sun can't be repaid.

登幽州台歌

陈子昂

前不见古人，
后不见来者。
念天地之悠悠，
独怆然而涕下。

登幽州台歌 卢甫圣 绘
On the Tower at Youzhou Painter: Lu Fusheng

On the Tower at Youzhou

Chen Zi' ang

Where are the great men of the past

And where are those of future years?

The sky and earth forever last;

Here and now I alone shed tears.

古意　丁小方 绘

Warriors and Songstress　Painter: Ding Xiaofang

古 意

李颀

男儿事长征，
少小幽燕客。
赌胜马蹄下，
由来轻七尺。
杀人莫敢前，
须如猬毛磔。
黄云陇底白云飞，
未得报恩不得归。
辽东小妇年十五，
惯弹琵琶解歌舞。
今为羌笛出塞声，
使我三军泪如雨。

Warriors and Songstress

Li Qi

Young men love to use force

Like swordsmen fond of strife.

They bet to win on horse,

Making light of their life.

They are brave in their fight

Like hedgehog with spikes black.

On the frontier white clouds and yellow clouds in flight,

Before the victory is won, they can't come back.

The Northeastern songstress is only fifteen years old,

Used to play on pipa, dance and sing with refrain.

She plays on flute now songs of the frontier so cold.

How can the warriors not shed copious tears like rain?

琴 歌

李颀

主人有酒欢今夕，
请奏鸣琴广陵客。
月照城头乌半飞，
霜凄万木风入衣。
铜炉华烛烛增辉，
初弹《渌水》后《楚妃》。
一声已动物皆静，
四座无言星欲稀。
清淮奉使千余里，
敢告云山从此始。

琴歌 丁小方 绘

Song of the Zither Painter: Ding Xiaofang

Song of the Zither

Li Qi

The host invites his guests to drink his happy wine,

And asks the zitherist to play a melody fine.

The moon shines on town walls and startles half the crows,

All the frost-bitten trees shiver when the wind blows.

The bronze censer appears brighter in candlelight,

The zitherist plays *Green Waves* and *the Princess Bright*.

When the music begins, silence reigns in the hall;

Fascinated by the song, shivering stars would fall.

The Northern messenger comes from so far away,

He seems to know the beauty of cloud since today.

听董大弹胡笳弄兼寄语房给事　丁小方 绘
Dong Playing a Homesick Song　Painter: Ding Xiaofang

听董大弹胡笳弄
兼寄语房给事

（选段）

李颀

蔡女昔造胡笳声，
一弹一十有八拍。
胡人落泪沾边草，
汉使断肠对归客。

……

董夫子，通神明，
深松窃听来妖精。
言迟更速皆应手，
将往复旋如有情。

……

川为静其波，
鸟亦罢其鸣。
乌珠部落家乡远，
逻娑沙尘哀怨生。

……

Dong Playing a Homesick Song

(Selected Verse)

Li Qi

Lady Cai wrote a homesick song in Tartar land,

And played its eighteen parts on pipe with her own hand.

The Tartars hearing it shed tears to wet the grass;

The envoy saw her part with broken heart, alas!

Master Dong plays on his pipa Lady Cai's song,

And fairies amid pines come to listen for long.

Hundreds of birds dispersed come together and stay,

For miles and miles floating clouds will not float away.

Waves in the stream are purified;

Birds will not twitter side by side.

The song reminds Han Princess' grief on leaving home,

And Tang Princess' lament when she began to roam.

听安万善吹觱篥歌

（选段）

李颀

南山截竹为觱篥，
凉州胡人为我吹。
傍邻闻者多叹息，
远客思乡皆泪垂。
枯桑老柏寒飕飗，
黄云萧条白日暗。
岁夜高堂列明烛，
美酒一杯声一曲。

听安万善吹觱篥歌　丁小方　绘
A Tartar Pipe　Painter: Ding Xiaofang

A Tartar Pipe

(Selected Verse)

Li Qi

The pipe is made of bamboo cut from southern mountains,

A Tartar from the northwest plays it low and high.

Those homesick travelers would shed tears like fountains;

The neighbors hearing it would utter sigh on sigh.

The wind whistles through mulberries and cypress old,

And dreary yellow clouds darken the bright sunny land.

When candles brighten the hall on New Year's Eve cold,

Why not enjoy the music with wine cup in hand?

夜归鹿门歌　朱敏　绘 ▶

Return to Deer Gate at Night　Painter: Zhu Min

岩扉松径长寂寥　唯有幽人自来去　辛卯年　敏

夜归鹿门歌

孟浩然

山寺钟鸣昼已昏，
渔梁渡头争渡喧。
人随沙岸向江村，
余亦乘舟归鹿门。
鹿门月照开烟树，
忽到庞公栖隐处。
岩扉松径长寂寥，
唯有幽人自来去。

Return to Deer Gate at Night

Meng Haoran

The temple bell tolls the knell of the parting day,

Noisy people at the ferry precipitate.

Along the shore to their village they wedge their way,

I go by boat to my hermitage at Deer Gate.

Moonbeams over the Gate shine on mist-shrouded trees;

I come to ancient hermitage as well as mine.

The solitude amid gate-like cliffs would please.

A hermit pacing freely on the path of pines.

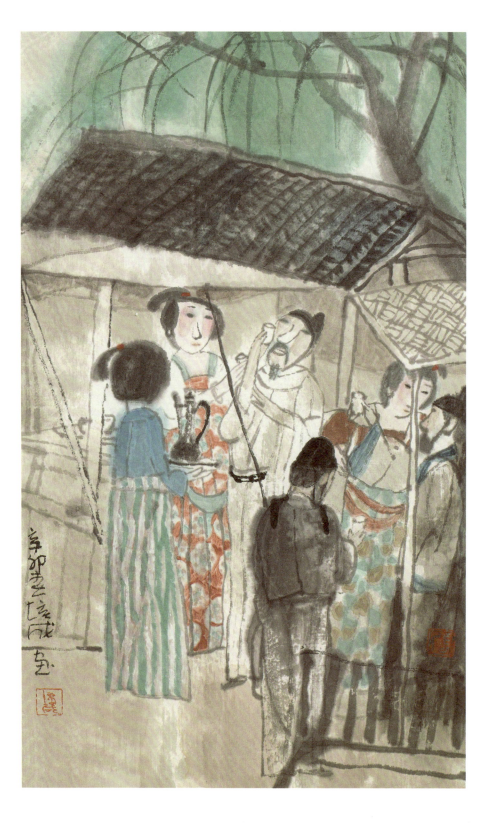

金陵酒肆留别

李白

风吹柳花满店香，
吴姬压酒劝客尝。
金陵子弟来相送，
欲行不行各尽觞。
请君试问东流水，
别意与之谁短长？

金陵酒肆留别　张培成 绘

Parting at a Tavern in Jinling Painter: Zhang Peicheng

Parting at a Tavern in Jinling

Li Bai

The tavern's sweetened when wind blows in willow-down,

A Southern maiden urges the guests to taste her wine.

My dear young friends have come to see me leave the town,

They who stay drink their cups and I who leave drink mine.

Oh, ask the river flowing to the east, I pray,

If he is happier to go than I to stay.

白雪歌送武判官归京　张培成 绘

Song of White Snow in Farewell to Secretary Wu Going Back to the Capital

Painter: Zhang Peicheng

白雪歌送武判官归京

岑参

北风卷地白草折，

胡天八月即飞雪。

忽如一夜春风来，

千树万树梨花开。

散入珠帘湿罗幕，

狐裘不暖锦衾薄。

将军角弓不得控，

都护铁衣冷难着。

瀚海阑干百丈冰，

愁云惨淡万里凝。

中军置酒饮归客，

胡琴琵琶与羌笛。

纷纷暮雪下辕门，

风掣红旗冻不翻。

轮台东门送君去，

去时雪满天山路。

山回路转不见君，

雪上空留马行处。

Song of White Snow in Farewell to Secretary Wu Going Back to the Capital

Cen Shen

Snapping the pallid grass, the northern wind whirls low;

In the eighth moon the Tartar sky is filled with snow.

As if the vernal breeze had come back overnight,

Adorning thousands of pear trees with blossoms white.

Flakes enter pearled blinds and wet the silken screen;

No furs of fox can warm us nor brocade quilts green.

The general cannot draw his rigid bow with ease;

E'en the commissioner in coat of mail would freeze.

A thousand feet o'er cracked wilderness ice piles,

And gloomy clouds hang sad and drear for miles and miles.

We drink in headquarters to our guest homeward bound;

With Tartar lutes, pipas and pipes the camps resound.

Snow in huge flakes at dusk falls heavy on camp gate;

The frozen red flag in the wind won't undulate.

At eastern gate of Wheel Tower we bid goodbye

On the snow-covered road to Heaven's Mountain high.

I watch his horse go past a bend and, lost to sight,

His track will soon be buried up by snow in flight.

丹青引 赠曹将军霸

（选段）

杜甫

……

先帝天马玉花骢，
画工如山貌不同。
是日牵来赤墀下，
迥立阊阖生长风。
诏谓将军拂绢素，
意匠惨澹经营中。
斯须九重真龙出，
一洗万古凡马空。

……

丹青引 赠曹将军霸　卢甫圣 绘

Pictures of Horses　Painter: Lu Fusheng

Pictures of Horses

(Selected Verse)

Du Fu

Piebald of Blooming Jade was the emperor's steed,

Many painters have pictured it, but none succeed.

When it was led before the flight of steps one day,

It outshone in the palace the dazzling array.

General Cao was ordered to paint it on the scroll,

As swift as wind, he tried to do with heart and soul.

When a dragon appears in the celestial sphere,

How dare a snake or serpent boast to be his peer!

观公孙大娘弟子舞剑器行　卢甫圣 绘

Dance of a Swordswoman　Painter: Lu Fusheng

观公孙大娘弟子舞剑器行

（选段）

杜甫

昔有佳人公孙氏，
一舞剑器动四方。
观者如山色沮丧，
天地为之久低昂。
爧如羿射九日落，
矫如群帝骖龙翔。
来如雷霆收震怒，
罢如江海凝清光。
……

Dance of a Swordswoman

(Selected Verse)

Du Fu

Gungsun was a fair swordswoman of bygone days,

Her sword dance marveled by all men shed dazzling rays.

The lookers-on stood still as mountains fascinated;

Even the azure sky and earth seemed agitated.

They were astonished as if nine suns were shot down;

The dance looked like a scene by dragons overflown.

The dancer came as fleet as angry thunder's roar,

And then it stopped as the sea raving no more.

石鱼湖上醉歌

元结

石鱼湖，似洞庭，
夏水欲满君山青。
山为樽，水为沼，
酒徒历历坐洲岛。
长风连日作大浪，
不能废人运酒舫。
我持长瓢坐巴邱，
酌饮四座以散愁！

石鱼湖上醉歌　卢甫圣　绘
Drinking on Stone Fish Lake　Painter: Lu Fusheng

Drinking on Stone Fish Lake

Yuan Jie

On Stone Fish Lake as on Dongting I gaze my fill.

On brimming summer water as on verdant hill.

Using the vale as cup and water as wine pools,

The tipplers sit on rocks as cosy as on stools.

The wind so strong has formed great waves from day to day:

It can't prevent the boats from bringing wine this way.

A ladle in my hand, I sit on rocky shore;

To do away with care, we drink the wine I pour.

桃源行　萧海春 绘
Song of Peach Blossom Land　Painter: Xiao Haichun

渔舟逐水爱山春，
两岸桃花夹古津。
坐看红树不知远，
行尽青溪忽值人。

王维《桃花源》句 原讨写之

桃源行

王维

渔舟逐水爱山春，两岸桃花夹古津。
坐看红树不知远，行尽青溪忽值人。
山口潜行始隈隩，山开旷望旋平陆。
遥看一处攒云树，近入千家散花竹。
樵客初传汉姓名，居人未改秦衣服。
居人共住武陵源，还从物外起田园。
月明松下房栊静，日出云中鸡犬喧。
惊闻俗客争来集，竞引还家问都邑。
平明闾巷扫花开，薄暮渔樵乘水入。
初因避地去人间，更问神仙遂不还。
峡里谁知有人事，世中遥望空云山。
不疑灵境难闻见，尘心未尽思乡县。
出洞无论隔山水，辞家终拟长游衍。
自谓经过旧不迷，安知峰壑今来变。
当时只记入山深，青溪几度到云林。
春来遍是桃花水，不辨仙源何处寻。

Song of Peach Blossom Land

Wang Wei

A fisherman loved vernal hills and winding stream,
His boat between the shores, he saw peach blossoms beam.
He knew not how far he'd gone, charmed by blooming scene,
Up to the end of the stream not a man was seen.
At the foot of a hill he found a winding way,
Beyond the hills a plain extended far, far away.
Viewed from afar, the forest seemed to scrape the sky,
Bamboos and flowers scattered in houses nearby.
A woodman told him a name used long, long ago,
People were dressed, in a style now no one would know.
As they had lived together in Peach Blossom Land,
Beyond the bustle fields were tilled with plough in hand.
Under moonlit pines cots looked quiet in the dark,
Up to sunlit clouds cocks' crow was heard with dogs' bark.
Curious about the stranger, people came from up and down,
Led him to their cottages and asked about the town.
Fallen petals on the lane were swept clean by day,
At dusk fishermen and woodsmen on homeward way.
Their fathers left the war-torn land to flee from woe,
This fairyland was found, away they would not go.
Deep in the vale, no one cared about world affair;
Gazing afar, they longed for cloud and mountain air.
Knowing not such fairy land was hard to be refound,
The fisherman longed to go back to his native ground.
He left the place and passed over mountains and streams,
But how could he forget the scene of his dear dreams?
He thought, having come once, he would not go astray,
Without knowing peak and stream would change on the way.
Last time he came, he only knew the mountain deep,
But memory of cloudy way he did not keep.
When spring came, everywhere he saw peach blossoms nice,
But where could he find again his lost paradise?

丽人行

杜甫

三月三日天气新，长安水边多丽人。

态浓意远淑且真，肌理细腻骨肉匀。

绣罗衣裳照暮春，蹙金孔雀银麒麟。

头上何所有？翠微匎叶垂鬓唇。

背后何所见？珠压腰衱稳称身。

就中云幕椒房亲，赐名大国虢与秦。

紫驼之峰出翠釜，水精之盘行素鳞。

犀箸厌饫久未下，鸾刀缕切空纷纶。

黄门飞鞚不动尘，御厨络绎送八珍。

箫鼓哀吟感鬼神，宾从杂遝实要津。

后来鞍马何逡巡，当轩下马入锦茵。

杨花雪落覆白蘋，青鸟飞去衔红巾。

炙手可热势绝伦，慎莫近前丞相嗔。

丽人行 韩硕 绘

Satire on Fair Ladies Painter: Han Shuo

Satire on Fair Ladies

Du Fu

The weather's fine in the third moon on the third day,
By riverside so many beauties in array.
Each of the ladies has a fascinating face,
Their skin is delicate, their manner full of grace.
Embroidered with peacocks and unicorns in gold,
Their dress in rich silks shines so bright when spring is old.
What do they wear on the head?
Emerald pendant leaves hang down in silver thread.
What do you see from behind?
How nice-fitting are their waist bands with pearls combined.
Among them there're the emperor's favorite kin,
Ennobled Duchess of Guo comes with Duchess of Qin.
What do they eat?
The purple meat of camel's hump cooked in green cauldron as a dish;
On crystal plate is served snow-white slices of raw fish.
See rhino chopsticks the satiated eaters stay,
And untouched morsels carved by belled knives on the tray.
When eunuchs' horses come running, no dust is raised;
They bring still more rare dishes delicious to the taste.
Listen to soul-stirring music of flutes and drums!
On the main road an official retinue comes.
A rider ambles on saddled horse, the last of all,
He alights, treads on satin carpet, enters the hall.
The willow-down like snow falls on the duckweed white;
The blue bird picking red handkerchief goes in flight.
The prime minister's powerful without a peer.
His angry touch would burn your hand. Do not come near!

送杜少府之任蜀州　施大畏 绘
Farewell to Prefect Du　Painter: Shi Dawei

送杜少府之任蜀州

王勃

城阙辅三秦，
风烟望五津。
与君离别意，
同是宦游人。
海内存知己，
天涯若比邻。
无为在歧路，
儿女共沾巾。

Farewell to Prefect Du

Wang Bo

You'll leave the town walled far and wide

For mist-veiled land by riverside.

I feel on parting sad and drear

For both of us are strangers here.

If you have friends who know your heart,

Distance cannot keep you apart.

At crossroads where we bid adieu,

Do not shed tears as women do!

题大庾岭北驿

宋之问

阳月南飞雁，
传闻至此回。
我行殊未已，
何日复归来？
江静潮初落，
林昏瘴不开。
明朝望乡处，
应见陇头梅。

题大庾岭北驿　车鹏飞 绘

At the Northern Post of the Peak of Mumes　Painter: Che Pengfei

At the Northern Post of the Peak of Mumes

Song Zhiwen

In the tenth moon wild geese south fly;

They will turn back at this peak high.

But I must farther southward go.

When may I come back? Do you know?

The river's calm when ebbs the tide;

Dense fog darkens the forest wide.

Tomorrow looking for my homeland,

I can only see mume trees stand.

潮平兩岸闊風正一帆懸

王灣詩

辛卯之夏嘉人

井曉孔風
童意

次北固山下

王湾

客路青山下，
行舟绿水前。
潮平两岸阔，
风正一帆悬。
海日生残夜，
江春入旧年。
乡书何处达，
归雁洛阳边。

Passing by the Northern Mountains

Wang Wan

My boat goes by green mountains high

And passes through the river blue.

The banks seem wide at the full tide;

A sail with ease hangs in soft breeze.

The sun brings light born of last night;

New spring invades last year that fades.

Where can I send word to my friend?

Homing wild geese, fly westward, please!

清晨入古寺
初日照高林
破山寺后禅院晓吆

题破山寺后禅院

常建

清晨入古寺，
初日照高林。
曲径通幽处，
禅房花木深。
山光悦鸟性，
潭影空人心。
万籁此皆寂，
惟闻钟磬音。

破山寺后禅院　林曦明 绘

A Buddhist Retreat behind an Old Temple in the Mountain Painter: Lin Ximing

A Buddhist Retreat behind an Old Temple in the Mountain

Chang Jian

I come to the old temple at first light,

Only tree-tops are steeped in sunbeams bright.

A winding footpath leads to deep retreat;

The abbot's cell is hid 'mid flowers sweet.

In mountain's aura flying birds feel pleasure;

In shaded pool a carefree mind finds leisure.

All worldly noises are quieted here;

I only hear temple bells ringing clear.

春望　韩硕 绘

Spring View　Painter: Han Shuo

春 望

杜 甫

国破山河在，
城春草木深。
感时花溅泪，
恨别鸟惊心。
烽火连三月，
家书抵万金。
白头搔更短，
浑欲不胜簪。

Spring View

Du Fu

On war-torn land streams flow and mountains stand;

In vernal town grass and weeds are overgrown.

Grieved over the years, flowers make us shed tears;

Hating to part, hearing birds breaks our heart.

The beacon fire has gone higher and higher;

Words from household are worth their weight in gold.

I cannot bear to scratch my grizzled hair;

It grows too thin to hold a light hairpin.

月 夜

杜甫

今夜鄜州月，

闺中只独看。

遥怜小儿女，

未解忆长安。

香雾云鬟湿，

清辉玉臂寒。

何时倚虚幌，

双照泪痕干。

月夜 戴敦邦 绘

A Moonlit Night Painter: Dai Dunbang

A Moonlit Night

Du Fu

On the moon over Fuzhou which shines bright,

Alone you would gaze in your room tonight.

I'm grieved to think our little children dear

Too young to yearn for their old father here.

Your cloudlike hair is moist with dew, it seems;

Your jade-white arms would feel the cold moonbeams.

O when can we stand by the window side,

Watching the moon with our tear traces dried?

天末怀李白

杜甫

凉风起天末，
君子意如何。
鸿雁几时到，
江湖秋水多。
文章憎命达，
魑魅喜人过。
应共冤魂语，
投诗赠汨罗。

Thinking of Li Bai from the End of the Earth

Du Fu

An autumn wind rises from the end of the sky.

What do you think of it in your mind and your eye?

When will the wild geese bring your happy news to me?

Could autumn fill the lake and the river with glee?

Good fortune never favors those who can well write;

Demons will ever do wrong to those who know what's right.

Would you confide to the poet wronged long ago

Your verse which might comfort his soul in weal and woe?

渡頭余落日墟里上孤煙 辛卯米敏

辋川闲居赠裴秀才迪

王维

寒山转苍翠，
秋水日潺湲。
倚杖柴门外，
临风听暮蝉。
渡头余落日，
墟里上孤烟。
复值接舆醉，
狂歌五柳前。

辋川闲居赠裴秀才迪　朱敏 绘
For My Outspoken Friend Pei Di in My Hermitage　Painter: Zhu Min

For My Outspoken Friend Pei Di in My Hermitage

Wang Wei

Cold mountains turn into deepening green,

Each day the autumn stream ripples with ease.

Out of my wicket gate on my staff I lean

To hear cicadas sing in evening breeze.

The setting sun beyond, the ferry half sunk,

The village smoke rises lonely and straight.

What joy to see my outspoken friend drunk,

Chanting to five willows before my gate!

山居秋暝 卢甫圣 绘

Autumn Evening in the Mountains Painter: Lu Fusheng

山居秋暝

王 维

空山新雨后，
天气晚来秋。
明月松间照，
清泉石上流。
竹喧归浣女，
莲动下渔舟。
随意春芳歇，
王孙自可留。

Autumn Evening in the Mountains

Wang Wei

After fresh rain in mountains bare,

Autumn permeates evening air.

Among pine trees bright moonbeams peer,

Over crystal stones flows water clear.

Bamboos whisper of washer-maids,

Lotus stirs when fishing boat wades.

Though fragrant spring may pass away,

Still here's the place for you to stay.

终南山

王维

太乙近天都，
连山到海隅。
白云回望合，
青霭入看无。
分野中峰变，
阴晴众壑殊。
欲投人处宿，
隔水问樵夫。

终南山 朱敏 绘
Mount Eternal South Painter: Zhu Min

Mount Eternal South

Wang Wei

The highest peak scrapes the blue sky;

It extends from hills to the sea.

When I look back, clouds veil the eye;

When I come near, I see mist flee.

Peaks change color from left to right,

Vales differ in shade or sunbeam.

Seeking a place to pass the night,

I ask a woodman across the stream.

过香积寺 朱敏 绘

The Temple of Incense Painter: Zhu Min

过香积寺

王维

不知香积寺，
数里入云峰。
古木无人径，
深山何处钟。
泉声咽危石，
日色冷青松。
薄暮空潭曲，
安禅制毒龙。

The Temple of Incense

Wang Wei

Where is the temple? I don't know.

Miles up to Cloudy Peak I go.

There's pathless forest in the dell.

Where deep in mountain rings the bell?

The rockside fountain seems to freeze;

Sunlight can't warm up green pine trees.

I sit in twilight by the pool,

To curb my desire I'd be cool.

送梓州李使君

王维

万壑树参天，
千山响杜鹃。
山中一夜雨，
树杪百重泉。
汉女输橦布，
巴人讼芋田。
文翁翻教授，
不敢倚先贤。

送梓州李使君　杨正新 绘
Seeing Li off to Zizhou　Painter: Yang Zhengxin

Seeing Li off to Zizhou

Wang Wei

The trees in your valley scrape the sky,

You'll hear in your hills cuckoo's cry.

If it rained at night in your mountain,

You'd see your tree tips hung like fountain.

Your women weave to make a suit;

You'd try to solve people's dispute.

The sage before you opened schools;

Like him you should carry out rules.

终南别业 朱敏 绘

My Hermitage in Southern Mountain Painter: Zhu Min

终南别业

王维

中岁颇好道，
晚家南山陲。
兴来每独往，
胜事空自知。
行到水穷处，
坐看云起时。
偶然值林叟，
谈笑无还期。

My Hermitage in Southern Mountain

Wang Wei

Following divine law after my middle age,

I live in Southern Mountain at my hermitage.

In joyful mood to wander, alone I would go

To find delightful scenes nobody else could know.

I'd go as far as the end of a stream or fountain

And sit and gaze on cloud rising over the mountain.

If I happen to meet with an old forest man,

We'd chat and laugh endlessly, as long as we can.

試寫孟浩然詩意 辛卯夏何㼐於海上

望洞庭湖赠张丞相

孟浩然

八月湖水平，
涵虚混太清。
气蒸云梦泽，
波撼岳阳城。
欲济无舟楫，
端居耻圣明。
坐观垂钓者，
徒有羡鱼情。

望洞庭湖赠张丞相 何曦 绘
On Dongting Lake Painter: He Xi

On Dongting Lake

Meng Haoran

The lake in the eighth moon runs high,

Its water blends with azure sky.

Cloud and dream fall into the river;

When its waves rise, the town walls shiver.

There's no boat for me to cross;

To go or not, I'm at a loss.

I watch the angler sitting still

And envy those who fish at will.

岁暮归南山 张培成 绘

Return to the Southern Hill by the End of the Year Painter: Zhang Peicheng

岁暮归南山

孟浩然

北阙休上书，
南山归敝庐。
不才明主弃，
多病故人疏。
白发催年老，
青阳逼岁除。
永怀愁不寐，
松月夜窗虚。

Return to the Southern Hill by the End of the Year

Meng Haoran

Don't write to North Imperial Court,

Go back to humble Southern cot!

Forsaken, of talent I'm short,

A poor sick man friends frequent not.

My white hair hasten my old age;

Bright spring days press the parting year.

Grief turns another sleepless page,

Into my room moon and pine peer.

待到重阳日
还来就菊花
孟浩人诗句
楚翘

过故人庄

孟浩然

故人具鸡黍，
邀我至田家。
绿树村边合，
青山郭外斜。
开轩面场圃，
把酒话桑麻。
待到重阳日，
还来就菊花。

过故人庄　张桂铭 绘

Visiting an Old Friend's Cottage　Painter: Zhang Guiming

Visiting an Old Friend's Cottage

Meng Haoran

My friend's prepared chicken and rice;

I'm invited to his cottage hall.

Green trees surround the village nice;

Blue hills slant beyond city wall.

Windows open to field and ground;

Over wine we talk of crops of grain.

On Double Ninth Day I'll come round

For the chrysanthemums again.

饯别王十一南游　车鹏飞 绘

Farewell to South-going Wang the Eleventh Painter: Che Pengfei

饯别王十一南游

刘长卿

望君烟水阔，
挥手泪沾巾。
飞鸟没何处，
青山空向人。
长江一帆远，
落日五湖春。
谁见汀洲上，
相思愁白蘋。

Farewell to South-going Wang the Eleventh

Liu Changqing

A broad stream shuts you out of sight;

I wave my hand, sleeves wet with tears.

Oh, where will stop the bird in flight?

In vain the green hill sad appears.

Your sail on the stream far away

Brings spring to the five lakes with speed.

The sun sheds its departing ray

On the heart-broken white reed.

白雲依靜渚 芳草閉閑門 辛卯 朱敏

寻南溪常道士

刘长卿

一路经行处，
莓苔见屐痕。
白云依静渚，
芳草闭闲门。
过雨看松色，
随山到水源。
溪花与禅意，
相对亦忘言。

寻南溪常道士 朱敏 绘

Visiting a Taoist by the Southern Creek Painter: Zhu Min

Visiting a Taoist by the Southern Creek

Liu Changqing

Going all the way to your place,

On the moss I see your foot-trace.

White clouds find in the pool a mate;

Green grass girts your leisurely gate.

After rain greener looks the mountain;

The pine-shaded path ends in a fountain.

Your heart and flowers' can be heard,

Understanding may need no word.

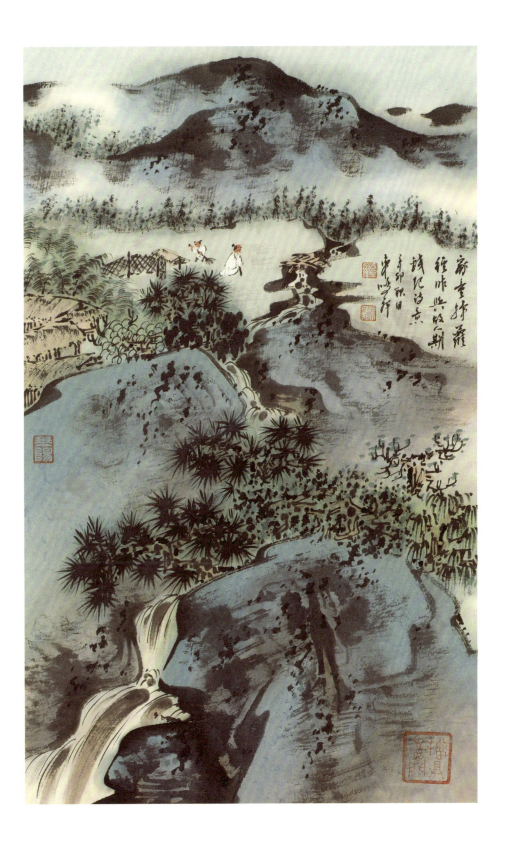

谷口书斋寄杨补阙

钱起

泉壑带茅茨，
云霞生薜帷。
竹怜新雨后，
山爱夕阳时。
闲鹭栖常早，
秋花落更迟。
家僮扫萝径，
昨与故人期。

Written to Censor Yang in My Study at the Mouth of the Vale

Qian Qi

My thatched cottage is girdled by winding streams,

Where rainbow clouds are born from ivy screen, it seems

The refreshing rain sees bamboos awake from dreams.

Mountains look lovelier in departing sunbeams.

The egrets often early go to roost at leisure,

And autumn flowers falling late would feel more pleasure.

I have told my houseboy to sweep clean the pathway.

To welcome you whom I invited yesterday.

江乡故人偶集客舍

戴叔伦

天秋月又满，
城阙夜千重。
还作江南会，
翻疑梦里逢。
风枝惊暗鹊，
露草泣寒虫。
羁旅长堪醉，
相留畏晓钟。

江乡故人偶集客舍 戴敦邦 绘

Meeting with a Friend in a Riverside Hotel Painter: Dai Dunbang

Meeting with a Friend in a Riverside Hotel

Dai Shulun

The moon in autumn shines so bright,

We've passed town on town, night by night.

Still we have met south of the stream,

We doubt if we are in a dream.

Winds startle magpies on the trees;

Weeping dew on grass, insects freeze.

We'll drink our fill in a hotel,

Afraid to hear the morning bell.

喜见外弟又言别 车鹏飞 绘

Meeting and Parting with My Cousin Painter: Che Pengfei

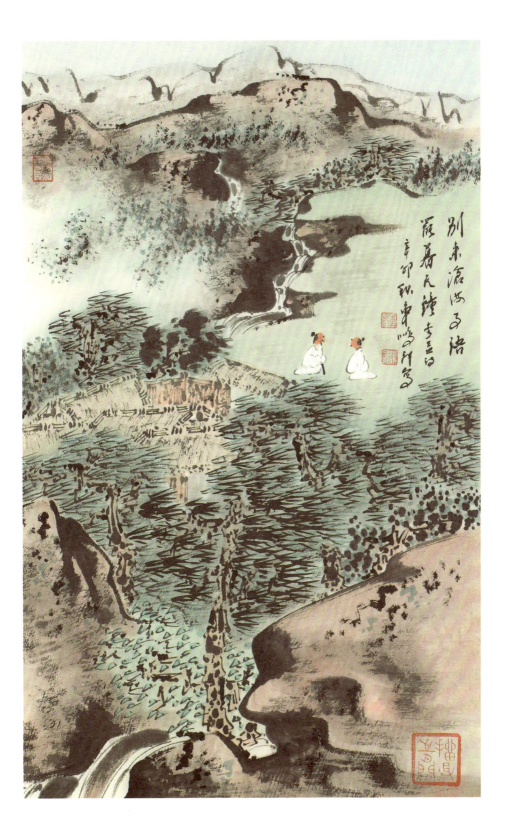

喜见外弟又言别

李益

十年离乱后，
长大一相逢。
问姓惊初见，
称名忆旧容。
别来沧海事，
语罢暮天钟。
明日巴陵道，
秋山又几重？

Meeting and Parting with My Cousin

Li Yi

We parted young for ten long years;

Not till grown up do we meet again.

At first I think a stranger appears;

Your name reminds me of your face then.

We talk of changes night and day

Until we hear the evening bell.

Tomorrow you'll go southward way

Over autumn hills, O farewell!

贼平后送人北归

司空曙

世乱同南去，
时清独北还。
他乡生白发，
旧国见青山。
晓月过残垒，
繁星宿故关。
寒禽与衰草，
处处伴愁颜。

贼平后送人北归　何曦　绘
Seeing a North-bound Friend Off Painter: He Xi

Seeing a North-bound Friend Off

Sikong Shu

In time of war we came to southern land;

Now peace restored, you return single-hand.

In alien place our hair has turned white;

At home again you'll see mountains upright.

The moon wanes to see fortress ruined of late;

The stars twinkle at ancient city gate.

What would your sad face see wherever you pass

But shivering birds and withering grass.

草 何曦绘

Grass Painter: He Xi

草

白居易

离离原上草，
一岁一枯荣。
野火烧不尽，
春风吹又生。
远芳侵古道，
晴翠接荒城。
又送王孙去，
萋萋满别情。

Grass

Bai Juyi

Wild grasses spread over ancient plain;

With spring and fall they come and go.

Fire tries to burn them up in vain;

They rise again when spring winds blow.

Their fragrance overruns the way;

Their green invades the ruined town.

To see my friend going away,

My sorrow grows like grass overgrown.

秋日赴阙题潼关驿楼

许浑

红叶晚萧萧，
长亭酒一瓢。
残云归太华，
疏雨过中条。
树色随关迥，
河声入海遥。
帝乡明日到，
犹自梦渔樵。

秋日赴阙题潼关驿楼 车鹏飞 绘

At the Western Pass on an Autumn Day Painter: Che Pengfei

At the Western Pass on an Autumn Day

Xu Hun

At dusk maple leaves fall shower by shower,

A cup of wine is drunk at parting hour.

The floating clouds return to Northern Peak,

A drizzling rain mingles with murmuring creek.

Beyond the Pass extend green tree on tree;

The roaring river would deafen the sea.

Tomorrow I'll be in capital town,

I'd like a woodman's life more than renown.

蝉 何曦 绘
To the Cicadas Painter: He Xi

蝉

李商隐

本以高难饱，
徒劳恨费声。
五更疏欲断，
一树碧无情。
薄宦梗犹泛，
故园芜已平。
烦君最相警，
我亦举家清。

To the Cicadas

Li Shangyin

High, you can't eat your fill;

In vain you wail and trill.

At dawn you hush your song;

The tree is green for long.

I drift as water flows,

And waste my garden grows.

Thank you for warning due,

I am as poor as you.

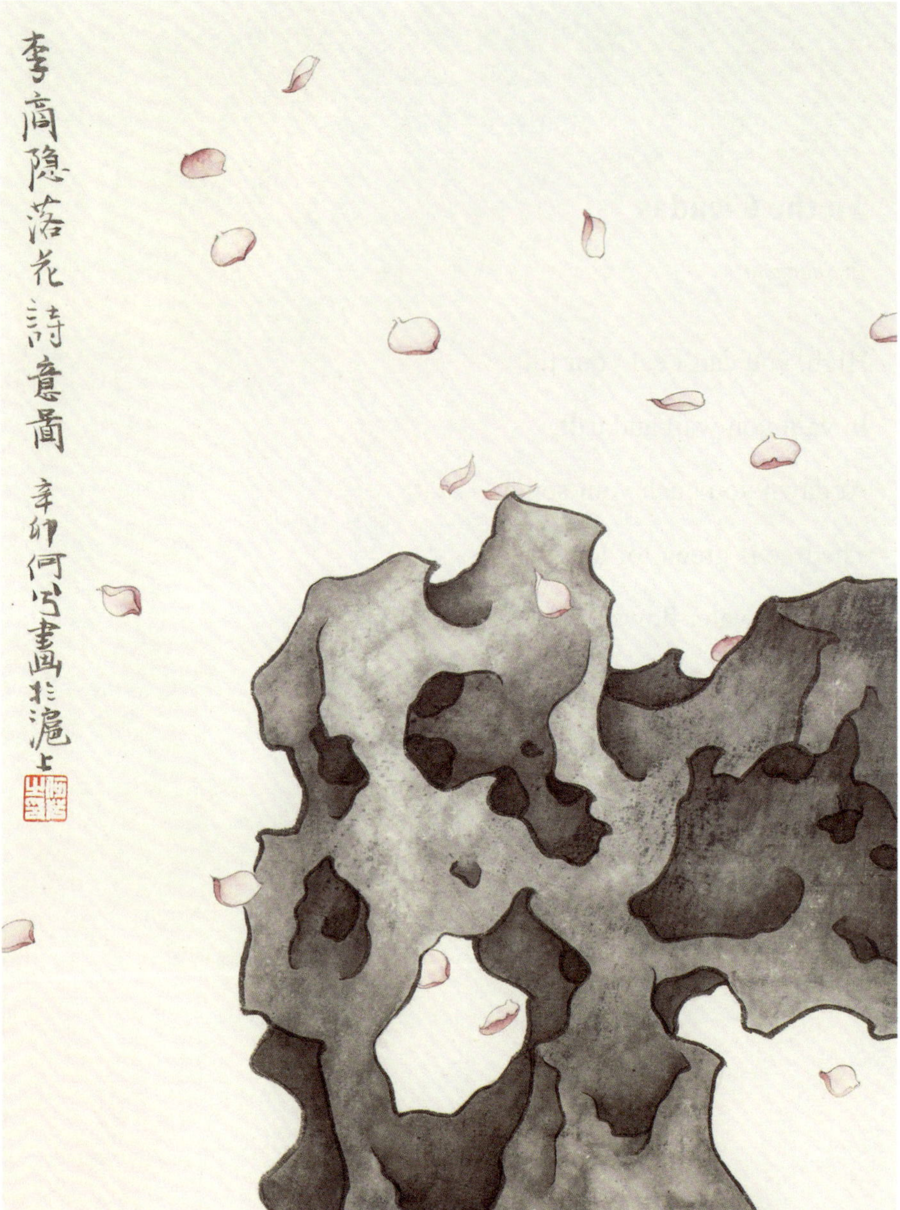

李商隱落花詩意畫

辛卯何�' 畫於滬上

落 花

李商隐

高阁客竟去，
小园花乱飞。
参差连曲陌，
迢递送斜晖。
肠断未忍扫，
眼穿仍欲归。
芳心向春尽，
所得是沾衣。

落花　何曦 绘
Falling Flowers Painter: He Xi

Falling Flowers

Li Shangyin

The guest has left my tower high,

My garden flowers pell-mell fly.

Here and there over the winding way

They say goodbye to parting day.

I won't sweep them with broken heart,

But wish they would not fall apart.

Their love with spring won't disappear,

Each dewdrop turns into a tear.

送人东游

温庭筠

荒戍落黄叶，
浩然离故关。
高风汉阳渡，
初日郢门山。
江上几人在，
天涯孤棹还。
何当重相见，
樽酒慰离颜。

Seeing a Friend Off to the East

Wen Tingyun

On dreary stream yellow leaves fly;

You leave old place with ideal high.

The autumn wind at ferry blows;

The rising sun on mountains glows.

How many friends on the stream wait

For you to come from far-off state?

When may I meet again with you

To drink good wine and not adieu?

灞原风雨定晚见雁行频辛卯米敏

灞上秋居

马戴

灞原风雨定，
晚见雁行频。
落叶他乡树，
寒灯独夜人。
空园白露滴，
孤壁野僧邻。
寄卧郊扉久，
何年致此身。

灞上秋居 朱敏 绘

Autumn in the Countryside Painter: Zhu Min

Autumn in the Countryside

Ma Dai

In countryside nor rain nor breeze,

At dusk I often watch wild geese.

From alien trees sear leaves in flight,

A lonely man by cold lamplight.

I hear in garden dripping dew,

My four walls know no neighbor new.

Lying long within wicket gate,

When can I perceive laureate?

寻陆鸿渐不遇　戴敦邦 绘

Visiting Lu Yu Without Meeting Him　Painter: Dai Dunbang

寻陆鸿渐不遇

皎然

移家虽带郭，
野径入桑麻。
近种篱边菊，
秋来未著花。
扣门无犬吠，
欲去问西家。
报道山中去，
归来每日斜。

Visiting Lu Yu Without Meeting Him

Jiao Ran

He moved not far away from the town,

A footpath leads to his mulberries.

Chrysanthemums by fenceside grown,

Not yet in bloom in autumn breeze.

I knock but no dog barks at the door,

I ask his neighbor in the west.

'Gone to the hill and seen no more,

At sunset he'll be back for rest.'

积雨辋川庄作

王维

积雨空林烟火迟，
蒸藜炊黍饷东菑。
漠漠水田飞白鹭，
阴阴夏木啭黄鹂。
山中习静观朝槿，
松下清斋折露葵。
野老与人争席罢，
海鸥何事更相疑。

积雨辋川庄作　杨正新 绘
Rainy Days in My Riverside Hermitage　Painter: Yang Zhengxin

Rainy Days in My Riverside Hermitage

Wang Wei

After long rain cooking fire's made late in the village;

Millet and greens are cooked for those doing tillage.

Over the boundless paddy fields egrets fly;

In gloomy summer forest golden orioles cry.

In quiet hills I watch short-lived blooms as I please,

And eat sunflower seeds under the green pine trees.

With other villagers I would not disagree:

Even sea gulls from far away would come near me.

客至　林曦明 绘

For a Friend Painter: Lin Ximing

客 至

杜甫

舍南舍北皆春水，
但见群鸥日日来。
花径不曾缘客扫，
蓬门今始为君开。
盘飧市远无兼味，
樽酒家贫只旧醅。
肯与邻翁相对饮，
隔篱呼取尽余杯。

For a Friend

Du Fu

North and south of my cottage winds spring water green;

I see but flocks of gulls coming from day to day.

The footpath strewn with fallen blooms is not swept clean;

My wicket gate is opened but for you today.

Far from market, I can afford but simple dish;

Being not rich, I've only old wine for our cup.

To drink with my neighbor if you wish,

I'll call him over the fence to finish the cup.

無邊落木蕭蕭下不盡長江滾滾來 辛卯 朱敏

登 高

杜甫

风急天高猿啸哀，
渚清沙白鸟飞回。
无边落木萧萧下，
不尽长江滚滚来。
万里悲秋常作客，
百年多病独登台。
艰难苦恨繁霜鬓，
潦倒新停浊酒杯。

登高　朱敏　绘
On the Height　Painter: Zhu Min

On the Height

Du Fu

The wind so swift, the sky so wide, apes wail and cry;

Water so clear and beach so white, birds wheel and fly.

The boundless forest sheds its leaves shower by shower;

The endless river rolls its waves hour after hour.

A thousand miles from home, I'm grieved at autumn's plight;

Ill now and then for years, alone I'm on this height.

Living in times so hard, at frosted hair I pine;

Cast down by poverty, I have to give up wine.

赠阙下裴舍人 萧海春 绘

For Secretary Pei of the Imperial Court Painter: Xiao Haichun

二月黄鹂飞上林
春城紫禁晓阴阴
长乐钟声花外尽
龙池柳色雨中深
钱起晚眺下裴云人许海生

赠阙下裴舍人

钱起

二月黄鹂飞上林，
春城紫禁晓阴阴。
长乐钟声花外尽，
龙池柳色雨中深。
阳和不散穷途恨，
霄汉常悬捧日心。
献赋十年犹未遇，
羞将白发对华簪。

For Secretary Pei of the Imperial Court

Qian Qi

In royal garden see orioles in vernal flight,

The morning clouds shed shades on the capital bright.

The happy palace bells are heard beyond the flowers;

The poolside willows look freshened after the showers.

But the sun has not warmed a poor heart aiming high,

Though I've tried my best to brighten the azure sky.

For ten years I've not won success by my word fair,

How dare I put the golden pin in my white hair?

遣悲怀（其二）

元稹

昔日戏言身后意，
今朝都到眼前来。
衣裳已施行看尽，
针线犹存未忍开。
尚想旧情怜婢仆，
也曾因梦送钱财。
诚知此恨人人有，
贫贱夫妻百事哀。

遣悲怀　戴敦邦　绘
To My Deceased Wife　Painter: Dai Dunbang

To My Deceased Wife (Ⅱ)

Yuan Zhen

'What if one of us should die?' we said for fun one day;

But now it has come true and passed before my eyes.

I can't bear to see your clothes and give them away;

I seal your embroidery lest it should draw my sighs.

Remembering your kindness, I'm kind to our maids;

Dreaming of your bounty, I give bounties as before.

I know there is no mortal but returns to the Shades,

But a poor couple like us have more to deplore.

无题 戴敦邦 绘

To One Unnamed Painter: Dai Dunbang

昨夜星辰昨夜风
画楼西畔桂堂东
李商隐无题诗意
戴敦邦作但恩多□□

无 题

李商隐

昨夜星辰昨夜风，
画楼西畔桂堂东。
身无彩凤双飞翼，
心有灵犀一点通。
隔座送钩春酒暖，
分曹射覆蜡灯红。
嗟余听鼓应官去，
走马兰台类转蓬。

To One Unnamed

Li Shangyin

As last night twinkle stars, as last night blows the breeze,

West of the painted bower, east of Cassia Hall.

Having no wings I can't fly to you as I please;

Our hearts at one, your ears can hear my inner call.

Maybe you're playing hook in palm and drinking wine

Or guessing what the cup hides under candle red.

Alas! I hear the drum call me to duties mine;

Like rootless weed to Orchid Hall I ride ahead.

利州南渡

温庭筠

澹然空水对斜晖，
曲岛苍茫接翠微。
波上马嘶看棹去，
柳边人歇待船归。
数丛沙草群鸥散，
万顷江田一鹭飞。
谁解乘舟寻范蠡，
五湖烟水独忘机。

利州南渡 车鹏飞 绘
Crossing the Southern River Painter: Che Pengfei

Crossing the Southern River

Wen Tingyun

The quiet river dyed in rays of setting sun,

The green islands and green mountains blend into one.

The horse neighs to see the boat go across the stream;

Roamers wait for ferries under willows in dream.

Flocks of gulls scatter over the reeds on the sand;

A heron flies across immense riverside land.

Who knows where to find the drunken sage in his boat?

On misty water of the five lakes he would float.

竹里馆 韩硕 绘

The Bamboo Hut Painter: Han Shuo

竹里馆

王 维

独坐幽篁里，
弹琴复长啸。
深林人不知，
明月来相照。

The Bamboo Hut

Wang Wei

Sitting among bamboos alone,

I play on lute and croon carefree.

In the deep woods where I'm unknown,

Only the bright moon peeps at me.

摩詰詩意圖　辛卯春何㦲畫於海上

相 思

王 维

红豆生南国，
春来发几枝。
愿君多采撷，
此物最相思。

相思 何曦 绘
Love Seeds Painter: He Xi

Love Seeds

Wang Wei

The red beans grow in southern land.

How many load in spring the trees?

Gather them till full is your hand;

They would revive fond memories.

杂诗 陈家泠 绘

Our Native Place Painter: Chen Jialing

杂 诗

王 维

君自故乡来，
应知故乡事。
来日绮窗前，
寒梅著花未？

Our Native Place

Wang Wei

You come from native place,

What happened there you'd know.

Did mume blossoms in face

Of my gauze window blow?

送崔九

裴迪

归山深浅去，
须尽丘壑美。
莫学武陵人，
暂游桃源里。

送崔九　车鹏飞 绘

Farewell to Cui the Ninth　Painter: Che Pengfei

Farewell to Cui the Ninth

Pei Di

You may go deep or not into the hill,

But you'd enjoy its beauty to the fill.

Don't imitate those who don't understand,

The happiness of the Peach Blossom Land!

终南望馀雪　朱敏 绘
Snow atop the Southern Mountains　Painter: Zhu Min

終南望餘雪

林表明霽色
城中增暮寒

终南望馀雪

祖咏

终南阴岭秀，
积雪浮云端。
林表明霁色，
城中增暮寒。

Snow atop the Southern Mountains

Zu Yong

How fair the gloomy mountainside!

Snow-crowned peaks float above the cloud.

The forest's bright in sunset dyed,

With evening cold the town's overflowed.

宿建德江

孟浩然

移舟泊烟渚，
日暮客愁新。
野旷天低树，
江清月近人。

宿建德江　张培成 绘

Mooring on the River at Jiande Painter: Zhang Peicheng

Mooring on the River at Jiande

Meng Haoran

My boat is moored near an isle in mist grey;

I'm grieved anew to see the parting day.

On boundless plain trees seem to scrape the sky;

In water clear the moon appears so nigh.

春晓　张桂铭 绘

A Spring Morning Painter: Zhang Guiming

春 晓

孟浩然

春眠不觉晓，
处处闻啼鸟。
夜来风雨声，
花落知多少。

A Spring Morning

Meng Haoran

This spring morning in bed I'm lying,

Not to awake till birds are crying.

After one night of wind and showers,

How many are the fallen flowers!

静夜思

李白

床前明月光，
疑是地上霜。
举头望明月，
低头思故乡。

静夜思 丁小方 绘
Thoughts on a Tranquil Night Painter: Ding Xiaofang

Thoughts on a Tranquil Night

Li Bai

Before my bed a pool of light—

O can it be frost on the ground?

Looking up, I find the moon bright;

Bowing, in homesickness I'm drowned.

怨情 朱新昌 绘

Waiting in Vain Painter: Zhu Xinchang

怨 情

李白

美人卷珠帘，
深坐颦蛾眉。
但见泪痕湿，
不知心恨谁。

Waiting in Vain

Li Bai

A lady fair uprolls the screen,

With eyebrows knit she waits in vain.

Wet stains of tears can still be seen.

Who, heartless, has caused her the pain!

登鹳雀楼

王之涣

白日依山尽，
黄河入海流。
欲穷千里目，
更上一层楼。

登鹳雀楼 丁小方 绘

On the Stork Tower Painter: Ding Xiaofang

On the Stork Tower

Wang Zhihuan

The sun along the mountain bows;

The Yellow River seawards flows.

You will enjoy a grander sight;

By climbing to a greater height.

蒼蒼竹林寺　杳杳鐘声晚荷笠
帶夕陽　青山独帰遠
辛卯夏日　甘肅晴瓜畫

送灵澈

刘长卿

苍苍竹林寺，
杳杳钟声晚。
荷笠带斜阳，
青山独归远。

Seeing off a Recluse

Liu Changqing

Green, green the temple amid bamboos,

Late, late bell rings out the evening.

Alone, he's lost in mountains blue,

With sunset his hat is carrying.

听弹琴

刘长卿

泠泠七弦上，
静听松风寒。
古调虽自爱，
今人多不弹。

听弹琴 韩硕 绘

Playing on Lute Painter: Han Shuo

Playing on Lute

Liu Changqing

How seven strings are clear and drear!

It's chilly breeze through pines we hear.

Lovely are ancient melodies;

The modern won't play them with ease.

听 筝

李端

鸣筝金粟柱，
素手玉房前。
欲得周郎顾，
时时误拂弦。

A Zitherist

Li Duan

How clear the golden zither rings,

When her fair fingers touch its strings!

To draw attention from her lord,

Now and then she strikes a discord.

三日入厨下
洗手作羹湯
未諳姑食性
先遣小姑嘗

王建《新嫁娘詞》意

戴敦邦畫于香竹簃

新嫁娘词

王建

三日入厨下，
洗手作羹汤。
未谙姑食性，
先遣小姑尝。

新嫁娘词 戴敦邦 绘
A Bride Painter: Dai Dunbang

A Bride

Wang Jian

Married three days, I go shy-faced,

To cook a soup with hands still fair.

To meet my mother-in-law's taste,

I send to her daughter the first share.

玉台体 韩硕 绘

Good Omens Painter: Han Shuo

玉台体

权德舆

昨夜裙带解，
今朝蟢子飞。
铅华不可弃，
莫是藁砧归？

Good Omens

Quan Deyu

My girdle fell loosened last night;

Today luck-spiders seen in flight.

Why not powder and paint my face

To greet the ungrateful with grace?

何满子

张祜

故国三千里，
深宫二十年。
一声《何满子》，
双泪落君前。

何满子　朱新昌 绘
The Swan Song　Painter: Zhu Xinchang

The Swan Song

Zhang Hu

Homesick a thousand miles away,

Shut in deep palace twenty years.

Singing the dying swan's sweet lay,

O how can she hold back her tears!

春 怨

金昌绪

打起黄莺儿，
莫教枝上啼。
啼时惊妾梦，
不得到辽西。

A Lover's Dream

Jin Changxu

Drive orioles off the tree

For their songs awake me

From dreaming of my dear

Far-off on the frontier!

哥舒歌

西鄙人

北斗七星高，
哥舒夜带刀。
至今窥牧马，
不敢过临洮。

哥舒歌 施大畏 绘
General Geshu Painter: Shi Dawei

General Geshu

Anonymous

When seven stars of the Plough are at their height,

General Geshu lifts his sword at night.

No more barbarians dare to come in force

To plunder us of our cattle and horse.

玉阶怨　卢甫圣 绘

Waiting in Vain on Marble Steps Painter: Lu Fusheng

坐
人
勇
攝
提
格
雷
萧
聖

玉阶怨

李白

玉阶生白露，
夜久侵罗袜。
却下水精帘，
玲珑望秋月。

Waiting in Vain on Marble Steps

Li Bai

The marble steps with dew turn cold.

Silk soles are wet when night grows old.

She comes in, lowers crystal screen,

Still gazing at the moon serene.

江南曲

李益

嫁得瞿塘贾，
朝朝误妾期。
早知潮有信，
嫁与弄潮儿。

江南曲 朱新昌 绘
A Southern Song Painter: Zhu Xinchang

A Southern Song

Li Yi

Since I became a merchant's wife,

I've in his absence passed my life.

A sailor comes home with the tide,

I should have been a sailor's bride.

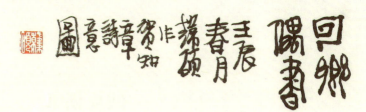

回鄉書

王辰春月蔣頌賀知章作詩意圖

回乡偶书

贺知章

少小离家老大回，
乡音无改鬓毛衰。
儿童相见不相识，
笑问客从何处来。

Home-Coming

He Zhizhang

I left home young and not till old do I come back,

Unchanged my accent, my hair no longer black.

The children whom I meet do not know who am I,

'Where do you come from, sir?' they ask with beaming eye.

闺 怨

王昌龄

闺中少妇不知愁，
春日凝妆上翠楼。
忽见陌头杨柳色，
悔教夫婿觅封侯。

闺怨 韩硕 绘

Sorrow of a Young Bride in her Boudoir Painter: Han Shuo

Sorrow of a Young Bride in her Boudoir

Wang Changling

The young bride in her boudoir does not know what grieves;

She mounts the tower, gaily dressed, on a spring day.

Suddenly seeing by roadside green willow leaves,

How she regrets her lord seeking fame far away!

江南逢李龟年　何曦 绘

Coming across a Disfavored Court Musician on the Southern Shore of the Yangzi River

Painter: He Xi

江南逢李龟年

杜甫

岐王宅里寻常见，
崔九堂前几度闻。
正是江南好风景，
落花时节又逢君。

Coming across a Disfavored Court Musician on the Southern Shore of the Yangzi River

Du Fu

How oft in princely mansions did we meet!

As oft in lordly halls I heard you sing.

Now the Southern scenery is most sweet,

But I meet you again in parting spring.

滁州西涧

韦应物

独怜幽草涧边生，
上有黄鹂深树鸣。
春潮带雨晚来急，
野渡无人舟自横。

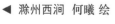

◀ 滁州西涧　何曦 绘

On the West Stream at Chuzhou　Painter: He Xi

On the West Stream at Chuzhou

Wei Yingwu

Alone I like the riverside where green grass grows

And golden orioles sing amid the leafy trees.

When showers fall at dusk, the river overflows;

A lonely boat athwart the ferry floats at ease.

月夜　何曦 绘 ▶

A Moonlit Night Painter: He Xi

月 夜

刘方平

更深月色半人家，
北斗阑干南斗斜。
今夜偏知春气暖，
虫声新透绿窗纱。

A Moonlit Night

Liu Fangping

The moon has painted half the room at dead of night,

The slanting Plough and Southern stars shed their dim light.

I can feel in the air the warm breath of new spring,

For through my window screen I hear the crickets sing.

春 怨

刘方平

纱窗日落渐黄昏，
金屋无人见泪痕。
寂寞空庭春欲晚，
梨花满地不开门。

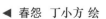

Loneliness

Liu Fangping

Through window screen she sees twilight of parting day,

Alone in gilded room, she wipes her tears away.

In lonely courtyard spring is growing desolate,

Pear-petals on the ground, she won't open the gate.

后宫词

白居易

泪湿罗巾梦不成，
夜深前殿按歌声。
红颜未老恩先断，
斜倚熏笼坐到明。

The Deserted

Bai Juyi

Her kerchief soaked with tears, she cannot fall asleep,

But overheard band music waft when night is deep.

Her rosy face outlasts the favor of the king;

She leans on her perfumed bed till morning birds sing.

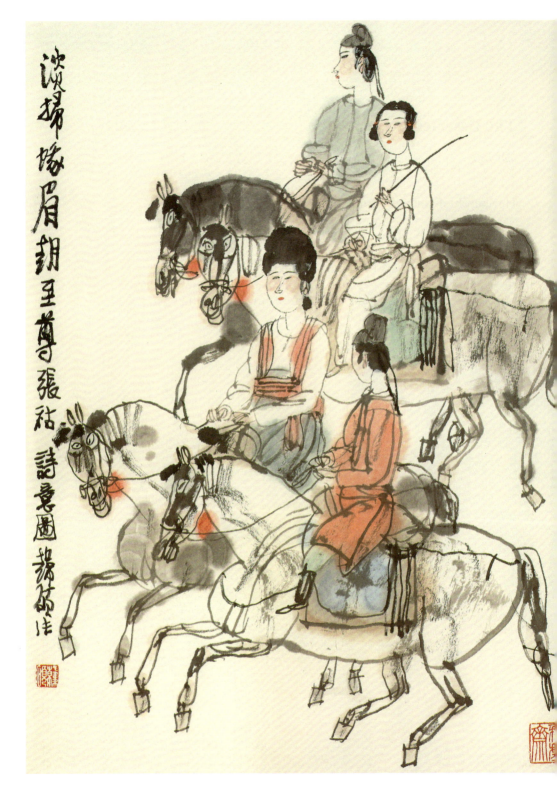

集灵台（其二）

张祜

虢国夫人承主恩，
平明骑马入宫门。
却嫌脂粉污颜色，
淡扫蛾眉朝至尊。

Long Life Terrace (Ⅱ)

Zhang Hu

The Duchess of Guo State had won imperial grace;

At dawn she rode through palace gates with dignity.

Disdainful of the paint which might have marred her face,

With lightly touched-up brows she met His Majesty.

宫中词 朱新昌 绘 ▶

Within the Palace   Painter: Zhu Xinchang

宫中词

朱庆馀

寂寂花时闭院门，
美人相并立琼轩。
含情欲说宫中事，
鹦鹉前头不敢言。

Within the Palace

Zhu Qingyu

The palace gate is closed, even flowers feel lonely;

Fair maidens side by side in shade of arbour stand.

They will complain of their lonesome palace life, only

Afraid the parrot might tell a tale secondhand.

秋 夕

杜牧

银烛秋光冷画屏，
轻罗小扇扑流萤。
天阶夜色凉如水，
卧看牵牛织女星。

◀ 秋夕 朱新昌 绘
An Autumn Night　Painter: Zhu Xinchang

An Autumn Night

Du Mu

The painted screen is chilled in silver candlelight,

She uses silken fan to catch passing fireflies.

The steps seem steeped in water when cold grows the night,

She lies watching heart-broken stars shed tears in the skies.

金谷园

杜牧

繁华事散逐香尘，
流水无情草自春。
日暮东风怨啼鸟，
落花犹似坠楼人。

The Golden Valley Garden

Du Mu

Past splendors are dispersed and blend with fragrant dust;

Unfeelingly rivers run and grass grows in spring.

At dusk the flowers fall in the eastern wind just

Like Green Pearl falling down and birds mournfully sing.

嫦 娥

李商隐

云母屏风烛影深，
长河渐落晓星沉。
嫦娥应悔偷灵药，
碧海青天夜夜心。

◀ 嫦娥 韩硕 绘
To the Moon Goddess Painter: Han Shuo

To the Moon Goddess

Li Shangyin

Upon the marble screen the candlelight is winking;

The Silver River slants and morning stars are sinking.

You'd regret to have stolen the miraculous potion;

Each night you brood over the lonely celestial ocean.

金陵图

韦庄

江雨霏霏江草齐，
六朝如梦鸟空啼。
无情最是台城柳，
依旧烟笼十里堤。

The Lakeside Land

Wei Zhuang

Over the riverside grass falls a drizzling rain;

Six Dynasties have passed like dreams, birds cry in vain.

Three miles along the dike unfeeling willows stand,

Adorning like a veil of mist the lakeside land.

清平调 _(其一)

李白

云想衣裳花想容，
春风拂槛露华浓。
若非群玉山头见，
会向瑶台月下逢。

◀ 清平调　卢甫圣 绘

The Beautiful Lady Yang　Painter: Lu Fusheng

The Beautiful Lady Yang（Ⅰ）

Li Bai

Her face is seen in flower and her dress in cloud,

A beauty by the rails caressed by vernal breeze.

If not a fairy queen from Jade-green Mountain proud,

She must be Goddess of the Moon a dreamer sees.

唐诗作者简介

张九龄（678—740）

字子寿，一名博物。韶州曲江(今广东韶关)人。长安二年(702)进士。官至中书侍郎同中书门下平章事。有《曲江集》。

李　白（701—762）

字太白，号青莲居士。祖籍陇西成纪（今甘肃静宁），生于西域碎叶。诗风雄奇豪迈，感情奔放，想象丰富，世称"诗仙"。有《李太白集》。

杜　甫（712—770）

字子美，祖籍襄阳，生于河南巩县（今河南巩义）。唐初诗人杜审言之孙。诗风沉郁顿挫，以古体、律诗见长，享有"诗圣"美誉。有《杜工部集》。

王　维（约701—761）

字摩诘，祖籍太原祁（今山西祁县）。开元九年（721）进士。官至尚书右丞。精通音律，擅长绘画，以山水田园诗著称。有《王右丞集》。

孟浩然（689—740）

以字行，襄州襄阳（今湖北襄樊）人。擅长五言律诗，诗风恬淡自然，意境清远。有《孟浩然集》。

王昌龄（？—约756）

字少伯，京兆长安（今陕西西安）人。开元十五年（727）进士。擅长七绝，风格凝炼，意境高远。《全唐诗》录存其诗四卷。明人辑有《王昌龄集》。

丘 为（约709—约804）

苏州嘉兴（今浙江嘉兴）人。天宝二年（743）进士，官至太子右庶子。擅长五言，属田园诗派。《全唐诗》录存其诗一卷，共计十三首。

常 建（708—约765）

长安（今陕西西安）人。开元十五年（727）进士。诗风清新。《全唐诗》录存其诗一卷。有《常建集》。

岑 参（约715—770）

江陵（今湖北荆州）人。天宝三年（744）进士。官至嘉州刺史。擅长七言，以边塞诗著称。有《岑嘉州诗集》。

元 结（719—772）

字次山，河南（今河南洛阳）人。天宝十二年（753）进士。官至容管经略使。诗风质朴平直。有《元次山文集》。

韦应物（约737—约791）

京兆万年（今陕西西安）人。后举进士，曾任苏州刺史。诗风高雅闲淡。有《韦苏州集》。

柳宗元（773—819）

字子厚。祖籍河东解（今山西运城）。贞元九年（793）进士。曾任礼部员外郎。"唐宋八大家"之一。其诗运思精密，呈峻洁澄澈境界。有《河东先生集》。

孟 郊（751—814）

字东野，湖州武康（今浙江德清）人。贞元十二年（796）进士。长于五言古诗，诗风瘦硬奇警，以苦吟著称。有《孟东野诗集》。

陈子昂（659—700）

字伯玉，梓州射洪（今四川射洪）人。开耀四年（684）进士。诗风高峻，为唐代诗文革新运动的先驱者。有《陈伯玉集》。

李 颀（？—753）

河南颍阳（今河南登封）人。开元二十三年（735）进士。擅长七言。《全唐诗》录存其诗三卷。有《李颀集》。

白居易（772—846）

字乐天，晚年号香山居士。祖籍太原，下邽（今陕西渭南）人。贞元十六年（800）进士，官至刑部尚书。与元稹共同倡导了"新乐府"运动。其诗风平易自然，深入浅出。有《白氏长庆集》。

李商隐（约813—约858）

字义山，号玉谿生，怀州河内（今河南沁阳）人。开成二年（837）进士。擅长七律和七绝，工于比兴，深于寄托。有《李义山诗集》。

王 勃（约650—676）

字子安，绛州龙门（今山西河津）人。"初唐四杰"之首。明人辑有《王子安集》。

宋之问（约656—约713）

一名少连，字延清。汾州西河（今山西汾阳）人，一说虢州弘农（今河南灵宝）人。上元二年（675）进士。擅长五律。《全唐诗》录存其诗三卷。明人辑有《宋之问集》。

王 湾（693—751）

洛阳人。先天元年(712)进士。官至洛阳尉。《全唐诗》录存其诗十首。

刘长卿（？—约789）

字文房。河间（今河北河间）人。天宝七年（748）进士。官终随州刺史。擅长五律。其诗气韵流畅，音调谐美。有《刘随州诗集》。

钱 起（约720—约782）

字仲文，吴兴（今浙江湖州）人。天宝九年（750）进士。官至考功郎中。"大历十才子"之一。擅长五言。有《钱考功集》。

戴叔伦（732—789）

字幼公，一作次公，润州金坛（今江苏金坛）人。官至容管经略使。《全唐诗》录存其诗三卷。明人辑有《戴叔伦集》。

李 益（748—约829）

字君虞。凉州姑臧（今甘肃武威）人。大历四年（769）进士。官至礼部尚书。擅长七绝，工乐府。《全唐诗》录存其诗二卷。有《李君虞集》。

司空曙（720—790）

字文明，一作文初，洺州（今河北永年）人。曾举进士，官至虞部郎中。"大历十才子"之一。《全唐诗》录存其诗二卷。有《司空文明诗集》。

杜 牧（803—853）

字牧之，京兆万年（今陕西西安）人。宰相杜佑之孙。大和二年(828)进士。官终中书舍人。擅长七绝，诗风明快豪放。有《樊川文集》。

许　浑（约791—约858）

字用晦，一作仲晦。润州丹阳（今江苏丹阳）人。大和六年（832）进士。其诗格调豪丽，句法圆稳工整，长于律诗。有《丁卯集》。

温庭筠（？—866）

本名岐，字飞卿，太原（今山西）人。官终国子助教。诗词兼工，其诗设色华丽，辞藻繁密。后人辑有《温庭筠诗集》和《金奁集》。

马　戴（799—869）

字虞臣，曲阳（今江苏东海）人。会昌四年（844）进士。官至国子博士。诗风壮丽，蕴藉自然，长于抒情写景的小诗。《全唐诗》录存其诗二卷。

韦　庄（约836—910）

字端己，长安杜陵（今陕西西安）人。韦应物四世孙。乾宁元年（894）进士。官至吏部侍郎兼平章事。诗风柔婉清丽。有《浣花集》。

皎　然（约720—？）

字清昼，本姓谢，湖州（今浙江长兴）人。唐名诗僧。擅长五言。有《皎然集》。

祖　咏（699？—746？）

洛阳（今河南洛阳）人。开元十二年（724）进士。《全唐诗》录存其诗一卷，共计三十六首。明人辑有《祖咏集》。

元　稹（779—831）

字微之，河南（今河南洛阳）人。官至同中书门下平章事。曾与白居易共同倡导"新乐府"运动，世称"元白"。有《元氏长庆集》。

裴　迪（716—？）

关中（今陕西）人。曾任蜀州刺史及尚书省郎。其诗多为五绝，以描摹山林为主。《全唐诗》录存其诗三十九首。

王之涣（688—742）

字季凌，晋阳（今山西太原）人，后徙绛。善边塞诗。《全唐诗》录存其诗六首。

李　端（约737—约784）

字正己，赵州（今河北赵县）人。大历五年(770)进士。官至杭州司马。"大历十才子"之一。擅七言，诗风直率。《全唐诗》录存其诗三卷。有《李端诗集》。

王　建（约767—约830）

字仲初，许州（今河南许昌）人。大历十年（775）进士。曾任陕州司马。以乐府诗见长，语言通俗，风格简约。有《王司马集》。

权德舆（759—818）

字载之，天水略阳（今甘肃秦安）人。官至礼部尚书同平章事。有《权德舆集》。

张　祜（约785—约852）

字承吉，贝州清河（今河北清河）人。其诗小巧约敛，以绝句见长。《全唐诗》录存其诗一卷。有《张承吉文集》。

金昌绪（生卒年不详）

临安（今浙江杭州）人。《全唐诗》仅录存其《春怨》诗一首。

西鄙人（生卒年不详）

《全唐诗》注云：天宝中歌舒翰为安西节度使，控地数千里，甚著威名，故西鄙人（西部边民）歌此。

贺知章（约659—约744）

字季真，越州永兴（今浙江萧山）人。证圣元年（695）进士，官至秘书监。其诗清新自然，善于造意。擅长绝句。《全唐诗》录存其诗一卷，共计十九首。

刘方平（？—约758）

河南（今河南洛阳）人。诗思悠远，以绝句见长。《全唐诗》录存其诗一卷，共计二十六首。

朱庆馀（797—？）

名可久，以字行。越州（今浙江绍兴）人。宝历二年（826）进士。其诗辞意清新，描写细致。擅长五律。《全唐诗》录存其诗二卷。有《朱庆馀诗集》。

About the Poets

Zhang Jiuling

A native of Shaozhou, Qujiang (present-day Shaoguan City, Guangdong Province), Zhang Jiuling (678-740) was also known as Zhang Bowu and Zishou (courtesy name). He passed the palace examination in 702, the 2nd year of the Chang'an period in the Tang Dynasty, and the highest position he held in the government was Vice Director of Secretariat (Jointly Manager of Affairs with the Secretariat-Chancellery). His poems are compiled into *Qujiang Ji*.

Li Bai

Born in Suiye in the Western Regions, Li Bai (701-762) was also called Taibai (courtesy name), or Qinglian Jushi (literary name) which literally means 'Blue Lotus Recluse'. His ancestral home was in Longxi, Chengji (present-day Jingning County, Gansu Province). In a vagarious and heroic style, his poems are imbued with fervent emotions and abundant imaginations. He is also hailed as 'Poet Immortal'. His poems are compiled into *Li Taibai Ji*.

Du Fu

Born in Gong County (present-day Gongyi City, Henan Province), Du Fu (712-770) was also known as Zimei (courtesy name) and his ancestral home was in Xiangyang City, Hubei Province. As the grandson of Du Shenyan, an early Tang poet, he was renowned for composing ancient-style and eight-line poems. His poems feature a depressed and rhythmic style. His works are compiled into *The Selected Poems of Du Fu*.

Wang Wei

Wang Wei (approx. 701-761) was also known as Mojie (courtesy name) and his ancestral home was in Taiyuanqi (present-day Qixian County, Shanxi Province). He passed the palace examination in 721, the 9th year of the Kaiyuan period in the Tang Dynasty and the highest position he held in the government was Assistant to Vice Director of the Department of State Affairs. Well versed in music and painting, he was particularly famous for composing pastoral poetry. His works are compiled into *Wang Youcheng Ji*.

Meng Haoran

A native of Xiangzhou, Xiangyang (present-day Xiangfan City, Hubei Province), Meng Haoran (689-740) was also known as Zixing (courtesy name). He excelled in composing five-character eight-line poems. His poetry features a natural style and pleasant spirit. His works are compiled into *Meng Haoran Ji*.

Wang Changling

A native of Jingzhao, Chang'an (present-day Xi'an City, Shaanxi Province), Wang Changling (?-about 756) was also known as Shaobo (courtesy name). He passed the palace examination in 727, the 15th year of the Kaiyuan period in the Tang Dynasty. He was good at writing seven-character four-line poems featuring a concise style and lofty spirit. His poems constitute four volumes of the *Complete Collection of Tang Poetry*. In the Ming Dynasty, his poems were also compiled into *Wang Changling Ji*.

Qiu Wei

A native of Suzhou Jiaxing (present-day Jiaxing City, Zhejiang Province), Qiu Wei passed the palace examination in 743, the 2nd year of the Tianbao period in the Tang Dynasty and the highest position he held in the government was Attendant to Prince. He excelled in writing five-character pastoral poems. Thirteen of his poems constitute one volume of the *Complete Collection of Tang Poetry*.

Chang Jian

A native of Chang'an (present-day Xi'an City, Shaanxi Province), Chang Jian (708-approx. 765) passed the palace examination in 727, the 15th year of the Kaiyuan period in the

Tang Dynasty. His poems feature a refreshing style. His poems are compiled into *Chang Jian Ji* and also constitute one volume of the *Complete Collection of Tang Poetry.*

Cen Shen

A native of Jiangling (present-day Jingzhou City, Hubei Province), Cen Shen (about 715-770) passed the palace examination in 744, the 3rd year of the Tianbao period in the Tang Dynasty and the highest position he held in the government was Prefect of Jiazhou. He excelled in writing seven-character poems on life in border areas. His works are compiled into *Cen Jiazhou Ji.*

Yuan Jie

A native of Henan (present-day Louyang City, Henan Province), Yuan Jie (719-772) was also known as Cishan (courtesy name). He passed the palace examination in 753, the 12th year of the Tianbao period in the Tang Dynasty, and the highest position he held in the government was Military Commissioner of Rongguan. His poems feature a plain and natural style. His works are compiled into the *Collection of Yuan Cisha's Works.*

Wei Yingwu

A native of Jingzhao Wannian (present-day Xi'an City, Shaanxi Province), Wei Yingwu (approx. 737-approx. 791) once served as Prefect of Suzhou after passing the palace examination. His poems feature an elegant and carefree style. His works are compiled into *Wei Suzhou Ji.*

Liu Zongyuan

Liu Zongyuan (773-819) was also known as Zihou (courtesy name) and his ancestral home was in Hedongxie (present-day Yuncheng City, Shanxi Province). He passed the palace examination in 793, the 9th year of the Zhenyuan period in the Tang Dynasty and once served as Vice Minister of Rites. As one of the 'Eight Great Prose Masters of the Tang and Song Dynasties', he is renowned for writing poems featuring a meticulously designed style and high spirit. His works are compiled into *Hedong Xiansheng Ji.*

Meng Jiao

A native of Huzhou Wukang (present-day Deqing County, Zhejiang Province), Meng Jiao (751-814) was also known as Dongye (courtesy name). He passed the palace examination in 796, the 12th year of the Zhenyuan period in the Tang Dynasty. He excelled in writing ancient-style five-character poems in a tough and peculiar style, thus being hailed as a painful-chanter poet. His works are compiled into the *Collection of Meng Dongye's Poems.*

Chen Ziang

A native of Zizhou, Shehong (present-day Shehong County, Sichuan Province), Chen Ziang (659-700) was also known as Boyu (courtesy name). He passed the palace examination in 684, the 4th year of the Kaiyao period in the Tang Dynasty. Famous for his lofty and serious style, he is one of the pioneers of the 'Classical Prose Movement in the Tang Dynasty'. His works are compiled into *Chen Boyu Ji.*

Li Qi

A native of Henan, Yingyang (present-day Dengfeng City, Henan Province), Li Qi (?-753) passed the palace examination in 735, the 23rd year of the Kaiyuan period in the Tang Dynasty. He excelled in composing seven-character poems. His works are compiled into *Li Qi Ji* and constitute three volumes of the *Complete Collection of Tang Poetry.*

Bai Juyi

A native of Xiagui (present-day Weinan City, Shaanxi Province) and with his ancestral home in Taiyuan, Bai Juyi (772-846) was also known as Letian (courtesy name) and Xiangshan Jushi (Recluse in Xiangshan Temple, literary name in his later years). He passed the palace examination in 800, the 16th year of the Zhenyuan period in the Tang Dynasty, and the highest position he held in the government was Minister of Justice. He led the 'New Yuefu Movement' with Yuan Zhen. His poems feature a plain and natural style as well as profound thoughts described in simple language. His works are compiled into *Baishi Changqing Ji.*

Li Shangyin

A native of Huaizhou, Henei (present-day Qinyang City, Henan Province), Li Shangyin (approx. 813 - approx. 858) was also known as Yishan (courtesy name) and Yuxisheng (literary name) which means the 'Lad by the Yuxi Stream'. He passed the palace examination in 837, the 2nd year of the Kaicheng period in the Tang Dynasty. He excelled in composing seven-character poems and using metaphors and symbols in his poems. His works are compiled into the *Collection of Li Yishan's Poems*.

Wang Bo

A native of Jiangzhou Longmen (present-day Hejin City, Shanxi Province), Wang Bo (approx. 650-676) was also known as Zi'an (courtesy name). He ranked among the 'Top Four Literary Eminences in the Early Tang Dynasty'. In the Ming Dynasty, his works were compiled into *Wang Zi'an Ji*.

Song Zhiwen

Song Zhiwen (approx. 656-approx. 713) was also known as Shaolian and Yanqing (courtesy name). He was a native of Fenzhou, Xihe (present-day Fenyang City, Shanxi Province) but some hold that he might be a native of Guozhou, Hongnong (present-day Lingbao City, Henan Province). He passed the palace examination in 675, the 2nd year of the Shangyuan period in the Tang Dynasty. He excelled in writing five-character eight-line poems. His poems constitute three volumes of the *Complete Collection of Tang Poetry*. In the Ming Dynasty, his works were compiled into *Song Zhiwen Ji*.

Wang Wan

A native of Luoyang City, Wang Wan passed the palace examination in 712, the 1st year of the Xiantian period in the Tang Dynasty and the highest position he held in the government was Commandant of Luoyang. Ten of his poems are included in the *Complete Collection of Tang Poetry*.

Liu Changqing

A native of Hejian (present-day Hejian City, Hebei Province), Liu Changqing (?-approx.

789) was also known as Wenfang (courtesy name). He passed the palace examination in 748, the 7th year of the Tianbao period in the Tang Dynasty, and the last position he held in the government was Prefect of Suizhou. He excelled in writing five-character eight-line poems featuring the masterful use of rhyme. His works are compiled into the *Liu Suizhou Ji*.

Qian Qi

A native of Wuxing (present-day Huzhou City, Zhejiang Province), Qian Qi (approx. 720-approx. 782) was also known as Zhongwen (courtesy name). He passed the palace examination in 750, the 9th year of the Tianbao period in the Tang Dynasty and the highest position he held in the government was Director of Merits Evaluation under the Ministry of Personnel. As one of the 'Ten Talents in the Dali Period', he excelled in writing five-character poems. His works are compiled into *Qian Kaogong Ji*.

Dai Shulun

A native of Runzhou, Jintan (present-day Jintan City, Jiangsu Province), Dai Shulun (732-789) was also known as Yougong or Cigong (courtesy name). The highest position he held in the government was Military Commissioner of Rongguan. His poems constitute three volumes of the *Complete Collection of Tang Poetry*. In the Ming Dynasty, his works were compiled into *Dai Shulun Ji*.

Li Yi

A native of Liangzhou, Guzang (present-day Wuwei City, Gansu Province), Li Yi (748-approx. 829) was also known as Junyu (courtesy name). He passed the palace examination in 769, the 4th year of the Dali period in the Tang Dynasty, and the highest position he held in the government was Minister of Rites. He excelled in writing seven-character four-line and Yuefu poems. His poems are compiled into *Li Junyu Ji* and constitute two volumes of the *Complete Collection of Tang Poetry*.

Sikong Shu

A native of Mingzhou (present-day Yongnian County, Hebei province), Sikong Shu was also known as Wenming or Wenchu (courtesy name). He passed the palace examination and the highest position he held in the government was Director of Logistics under the Ministry of Works. He was one of the 'Ten Talents in the Dali Period'. His works are compiled into the *Collection of Sikong Wenming's Poems* and constitute two volumes of the *Complete Collection of Tang Poetry*.

Du Mu

A native of Jingzhao, Wannian (present-day Xi'an City, Shaanxi province), Du Mu (803-853) was also known as Muzhi (courtesy name). As the grandson of Grand Councilor Du You, he passed the palace examination in 828, the 2nd year of the Dahe period in the Tang Dynasty, and the last position he held in the government was Secretariat Drafter. He excelled in writing seven-character four-line poems featuring an uplifting and bold style. His works are compiled into the *Collection of F's Works*.

Xu Hun

A native of Runzhou, Danyang (present-day Danyang City, Jiangsu Province), Xu Hun was also known as Yonghui or Zhonghui (courtesy name). He passed the palace examination in 832, the 6th year of the Dahe period in the Tang Dynasty. He was skilled at writing eight-line poems featuring a magnificent style and neat structures. His poems are compiled into *Ding Mao Ji*.

Wen Tingyun

A native of Taiyuan (present-day Taiyuan City, Shanxi Province), Wen Tingyun (?-866) was also known as Wen Qi (original name) or Feiqing (courtesy name). The last position he held in the government was Instructor at the School for the Sons of the State under the Directorate of Education. He excelled in writing both poems and lyrics featuring a gorgeous style and complicated expressions. His works are compiled into the *Collection of Wen Tingyun's Poems* and *Jin Lian Ji*.

Ma Dai

A native of Quyang (present-day Donghai County, Jiangsu Province), Ma Dai was also known as Yuchen (courtesy name). He passed the palace examination in 844, the 4th year of the Huichang period in the Tang Dynasty, and the highest position he held in the government was Erudite at the School for the Sons of the State under the Directorate of Education. He excelled in writing lyric and scenery poetry featuring a gorgeous style and a focus on natural beauty. His poems constitute two volumes of the *Complete Collection of Tang Poetry*.

Wei Zhuang

A native of Chang'an, Duling (present-day Xi'an City, Shaanxi Province), Wei Zhuang (approx. 836-910) was also known as Duanji (courtesy name). As the great-grandson of Wei Yingwu (a famous Tang poet), he passed the palace examination in 894, the 1st year of the Qianning period in the Tang Dynasty, and the highest position he held in the government was Vice Director at the Ministry of Personnel (concurrently Manager of Affairs). His poems, featuring a graceful style, are compiled into *Huan Hua Ji*.

Jiao Ran

A native of Huzhou (present-day Changxing County, Zhejiang Province), Jiao Ran (approx. 720-?) was also known as Xie Ran (original name) and Qingzhou (courtesy name). A famous monk poet in the Tang Dynasty, he excelled in writing five-character poems. His works are compiled into *Jiao Ran Ji*.

Zu Yong

A native of Luoyang (present-day Luoyang City, Henan province), Zu Yong (699?-746?) passed the palace examination in 724, the 12th year of the Kaiyuan period in the Tang Dynasty. Thirty-six of his poems constitute one volume of the *Complete Collection of Tang Poetry*. In the Ming Dynasty, his works were compiled into *Zu Yong Ji*.

Yuan Zhen

A native of Luoyang (present-day Luoyang City, Henan Province), Yuan Zhen (779-831) was also known as Weizhi (courtesy name). The highest position he held in the government was Manager of Affairs with the Secretariat-Chancellery. He led the 'New

Yuefu Movement' with Bai Juyi. The two poets are hailed as 'Yuan Bai'. His works are compiled into *Yuanshi Changqing Ji*.

Pei Di

A native of Guanzhong (present-day Shaanxi Province), Pei Di (716-?) served successively as Prefect of Shuzhou and Director at the Department of State Affairs. Most of his works are five-character four-line poems depicting mountains and forests. Thirty-nine of his poems are included into the Complete *Collection of Tang Poetry*.

Wang Zhihuan

Also known as Jiling (courtesy name), Wang Zhihuan (688-742) was a native of Jinyang (present-day Taiyuan City, Shanxi Province) and later moved to Jiangzhou. He was skilled at writing poems on life in border areas. Six of his poems are included in the *Complete Collection of Tang Poetry*.

Li Duan

A native of Zhaozhou (present-day Zhaoxian County, Hebei Province), Li Duan was also known as Zhengji (courtesy name). He passed the palace examination in 770, the 5th year of the Dali period in the Tang Dynasty, and the highest position he held in the government was Prefect of Hangzhou. As one of the 'Ten Talents in the Dali Period', he excelled in writing seven-character poems featuring a plain and simple style. His works are compiled into the *Collection of Li Duan's Poems* and constitute three volumes of the *Complete Collection of Tang Poetry*.

Wang Jian

A native of Xuzhou (present-day Xuchang City, Henan Province), Wang Jian (approx. 767-approx. 830) was also known as Zhongchu (courtesy name). He passed the palace examination in 775, the 10th year of the Dali period in the Tang Dynasty, and once served as Prefect of Shanzhou. He excelled in composing Yuefu poems featuring a concise style and simple language. His works are compiled into *Wang Sima Ji*.

Quan Deyu

A native of Tianshui Lueyang (present-day Qin'an County, Gansu Province), Quan Deyu (759-818) was also known as Zaizhi (courtesy name). The highest position he held in the government was Minister of Rites (Jointly Manager of Affairs). His works are compiled into *Quan Deyu Ji*.

Zhang Hu

A native of Beizhou, Qinghe (present-day Qinghe County, Hebei Province), Zhang Hu (approx. 785-approx. 852) was also known as Chengji (courtesy name). He excelled in writing four-line poems featuring a concise and implicit style. His poems are compiled into the *Collection of Zhang Chengji's Works* and constitute one volume of the *Complete Collection of Tang Poetry*.

Jin Changxu

Jin Changxu was a native of Lin'an (present-day Hangzhou City, Zhejiang Province). His poem titled 'Chun Yuan' (Sadness in Spring) is included into the *Complete Collection of Tang Poetry*.

The Xibiren (lower-class people living in Northwestern Region of ancient China)

According to the notes in the *Complete Collection of Tang Poetry*, as the Military Commissioner of the frontier Anxi region in the mid-Tianbao period of the Tang Dynasty, Ge Shuhan was well-known for his control over lands spanning thousands of miles. Therefore local people created the song to extol him.

He Zhizhang

A native of Yuezhou, Yongxing (present-day Xiaoshan District, Hangzhou City, Zhejiang Province), He Zhizhang (approx. 659-approx. 744) was also known as Jizhen (courtesy name). He passed the palace examination in 695, the 1st year of the Zhengsheng period in the Tang Dynasty, and the highest position he held in the government was Supervisor of Books. He excelled in writing four-line poems featuring a refreshing and natural style. Nineteen of his poems constitute one volume of the *Complete Collection of Tang Poetry*.

Liu Fangping

Liu Fangping was a native of Luoyang (present-day Luoyang City, Henan Province). He was famous for writing four-line poems featuring thought-provoking ideas. Twenty-six of his poems constitute one volume of the *Complete Collection of Tang Poetry*.

Zhu Qingyu

A native of Yuezhou (present-day Shaoxing City, Zhejiang Province), Zhu Qingyu (797-?) was usually known by his courtesy name and his original name was Kejiu. He passed the palace examination in 826, the 2nd year of the Baoli period in the Tang Dynasty. He excelled in writing five-character eight-line poems featuring refreshing ideas and detailed depictions. His works are compiled into the *Collection of Zhu Qingyu's Poems* and constitute two volumes of the *Complete Collection of Tang Poetry*.

绘画作者简介

陈佩秋（女，1923年生）

河南南阳人。毕业于杭州国立艺术专科学校。上海中国画院画师，上海市文史研究馆馆员，中国美术家协会会员，上海市美术家协会荣誉顾问，上海中国画院顾问，上海大学美术学院兼职教授，上海书画院院长，海上印社社长。

林曦明（1926年生）

浙江永嘉人。上海中国画院画师，上海市文史研究馆馆员，中国美术家协会会员，上海大学美术学院兼职教授。曾任中国剪纸学会名誉会长、上海剪纸学会会长。

陈家泠（1937年生）

浙江杭州人。毕业于浙江美术学院。上海中国画院画师，中国美术家协会会员，上海大学美术学院教授，中国国家画院研究员。

戴敦邦（1938年生）

江苏镇江人。毕业于上海第一师范学校。上海中国画院画师，中国美术家协会会员，上海交通大学教授。

张桂铭（1939—2014年）

浙江绍兴人。毕业于浙江美术学院。上海中国画院画师，中国美术家协会会员，中国国家画院研究员。曾任上海中国画院副院长、刘海粟美术馆执行馆长。

韩天衡（1940年生）

江苏苏州人。上海中国画院画师，西泠印社副社长，上海韩天衡文化艺术基金会理事长，中国篆刻艺术院名誉院长，中国美术家协会会员，上海中国画院顾问，上海交通大学兼职教授。曾任中国篆刻艺术院院长，中国书法家协会篆刻艺术委员会副主任，上海市书法家协会副主席，上海中国画院副院长。

杨正新（1942年生）

上海人。毕业于上海美术专科学校。上海中国画院画师，中国美术家协会会员，上海大学美术学院兼职教授。

萧海春（1944年生）

江西丰城人。毕业于上海工艺美术学校。上海中国画院画师，中国工艺美术大师，上海市美术家协会会员。

韩　硕（1945年生）

浙江杭州人。毕业于上海大学美术学院。上海中国画院画师，上海大学美术学院兼职教授，上海中国画院艺委会主任，中国画学会副会长。曾任上海中国画院副院长，中国美术家协会理事。

张培成（1948年生）

江苏太仓人。上海中国画院画师，中国美术家协会会员，上海大学美术学院兼职教授。曾任刘海粟美术馆执行馆长，上海市美术家协会副主席。

卢甫圣（1949年生）

浙江东阳人。毕业于浙江美术学院。上海中国画院画师，上海市文史研究馆馆员，中国美术学院兼职教授。曾任中国美术家协会理事、上海市美术家协会副主席、上海书画出版社总编辑。

施大畏（1950年生）

浙江湖州人。毕业于上海大学美术学院。上海大学美术学院兼职教授，中国国家画院院委兼研究员，上海中国画院院长，全国政协委员。曾任中国美术家协会副主席，上海市文联主席、上海市美术家协会主席。

车鹏飞（1951年生）

山东莱阳人。毕业于上海师范大学。上海中国画院画师，中国美术家协会会员。曾任上海市美术家协会常务理事，上海中国画院副院长。

朱新昌（1954年生）

浙江宁波人。毕业于上海师范大学。上海中国画院画师，中国美术家协会会员，上海市美术家协会理事。

马小娟（女，1955年生）

江苏南京人。毕业于浙江美术学院。上海中国画院画师，中国美术家协会会员，上海市美术家协会常务理事。

朱　敏（1956年生）

浙江新昌人。毕业于浙江美术学院。上海中国画院画师，上海市美术家协会理事。

丁小方（1957年生）

浙江绍兴人。毕业于上海大学美术学院。上海中国画院画师，中国美术家协会会员，上海市美术家协会理事。

何曦（1960 年生）

浙江嘉兴人。毕业于浙江美术学院。上海中国画院画师、创研室主任，中国美术家协会会员，上海市美术家协会常务理事。

About the Painters

Chen Peiqiu

Chen Peiqiu, born in 1923, is a native of Nanyang, Henan Province. Chen graduated from the Economics Department of National Southwest Associated University and the National Art School. She serves as Art Advisor to Shanghai Chinese Painting Academy, holding the title of Level-1 Artist. Chen is a member of China Artists Association and Shanghai Research Institute of Culture and History, an honorary Advisor to Shanghai Artists Association and Advisor to Shanghai Calligraphers Association. She also works as an adjunct professor at the College of Fine Arts, Shanghai University.

Lin Ximing

Lin Ximing, born in 1925, is a native of Yongjia, Zhejiang Province. Former painter with Shanghai Chinese Painting Academy, he retired in 1996. He is a member of China Artists Association, and an adjunct professor of the College of Fine Arts, Shanghai University, holding the title of Level-1 Artist.

Chen Jialing

Chen Jialing, born in 1937, is a native of Hangzhou, Zhejiang Province. Graduating from the Traditional Chinese Painting Department of Zhejiang Academy of Fine Arts, he is now an adjunct painter with Shanghai Chinese Painting Academy, member of China Artists Association and Shanghai Artists Association, and professor of the College of Fine Arts, Shanghai University.

Dai Dunbang

Dai Dunbang, born in 1938, is a native of Zhenjiang, Jiangsu Province. He is an adjunct painter with Shanghai Chinese Painting Academy, a member of China Artists Association and Vice-Director of its Comic Strips Council. He also serves as Executive Director of

Shanghai Artists Association and a professor of Shanghai Jiao Tong University.

Zhang Guiming

Zhang Guiming, born in 1939, is a native of Shaoxing, Zhejiang Province. Graduating from the Traditional Chinese Painting Department of Zhejiang Academy of Fine Arts, he is an adjunct painter with Shanghai Chinese Painting Academy and a member of its Art Council, holding the title of Level-1 Artist. He is also a member of China Artists Association, Shanghai Artists Association, Shanghai Calligraphers Association and Shanghai Federation of Literary and Art Circles. He is awarded the special allowance by the State Council.

Han Tianheng

Han Tianheng, born in 1940, is a native of Suzhou, Jiangsu Province. Han is Art Advisor to Shanghai Chinese Painting Academy, holding the title of Level-1 Artist, and President of Chinese Academy of Seal Engraving. He is also a member of China Artists Association, Shanghai Artists Association, and Shanghai Federation of Literary and Art Circles. He also holds the positions of Vice-director of the Seal Engraving Council of China Calligraphers Association, Chief Advisor to Shanghai Calligraphers Association, and is a professor of the Graduate School of Chinese Social Science Academy, and an adjunct professor of Shanghai Jiao Tong University. He is a recipient of the special allowance granted by the State Council.

Yang Zhengxin

Yang Zhengxin, born in 1942, is a native of Shanghai. Graduating from Shanghai Fine Arts School, he now works as a painter with Shanghai Chinese Painting Academy and is a member of its Art Council, holding the title of Level-1 Artist. He is also a member of China Artists Association and Shanghai Artists Association, and an adjunct professor of the College of Fine Arts, Shanghai University.

Xiao Haichun

Xiao Haichun, born in 1944, is a native of Fengcheng, Jiangxi Province. Graduating from Shanghai Arts and Crafts School, he works now as an adjunct painter with Shanghai

Chinese Painting Academy, and is a master of arts and crafts. He is also a member of Shanghai Artists Association and its Traditional Chinese Painting Committee.

Han Shuo

Han Shuo, born in 1945, is a native of Hangzhou, Zhejiang Province, and a graduate of the Traditional Chinese Painting Department of the College of Fine Arts, Shanghai University. Former Vice-President of Shanghai Chinese Painting Academy, he now works as a painter with Shanghai Chinese Painting Academy and Director of its Art Committee, holding the title of Level-1 Artist. He is also Director of China Artists Association and a member of its Traditional Chinese Painting Committee. He also holds the positions of Vice-President of Chinese Painting Institute, Executive Director of Shanghai Artists Association and Director of its Traditional Chinese Painting Committee, and is an adjunct professor of the College of Fine Arts, Shanghai University. He is a recipient of the special allowance granted by the State Council.

Zhang Peicheng

Zhang Peicheng, born in 1948, is a native of Taicang, Jiangsu Province. He works as an adjunct painter with Shanghai Chinese Painting Academy and Vice-Director of its Art Council, holding the title of Level-1 Artist. He is also a member of China Artists Association, Vice-Chairman of Shanghai Artists Association and a member of its Traditional Chinese Painting Council, and an adjunct professor of the College of Fine Arts, Shanghai University.

Lu Fusheng

Lu Fusheng, born in 1949, is a native of Dongyang, Zhejiang Province and a graduate of Zhejiang Academy of Fine Arts. He works as an adjunct painter with Shanghai Chinese Painting Academy and Vice-Director of its Art Council. He is also Director of China Artists Association, Vice-Chairman of Shanghai Artists Association, and President and Chief-editor of Shanghai Literature & Art Publishing House. He is a member of Shanghai Committee of the Chinese People's Political Consultative Conference and Shanghai Federation of Literary and Art Circles, and a PhD supervisor of China Academy of Art.

Shi Dawe

Shi Dawei, born in 1950, is a native of Huzhou, Zhejiang Province, and a graduate of the Traditional Chinese Painting Department of the College of Fine Arts, Shanghai University. He is Vice-Inspector of Shanghai Municipal Administration of Culture, Radio, Film and TV and President of Shanghai Chinese Painting Academy, holding the title of Level-1 Artist. He is also a member of the National Committee of Chinese People's Political Consultative Conference, and Vice-Chairman of China Artists Association. He is Chairman of Shanghai Federation of Literary and Art Circles and Shanghai Artists Association, and Director of Shanghai Lin Fengmian Research Institute. He also serves as an adjunct professor at the College of Fine Arts, Shanghai University and a guest professor of Shanghai Institute of Visual Art, Fudan University. He is awarded the special allowance by the State Council.

Che Pengfei

Che Pengfei, born in 1951, is a native of Laiyang, Shandong Province, and a graduate of Shanghai Normal University. Former Vice-President of Shanghai Chinese Painting Academy, he works as a painter with Shanghai Chinese Painting Academy and is a member of its Art Council, holding the title of Level-1 Artist. He is also a member of China Artists Association, Executive Director of Shanghai Artists Association and a member of its Traditional Chinese Painting Council.

Zhu Xinchang

Zhu Xinchang, born in 1954, native of Ningbo, Zhejiang Province, graduated from the Fine Arts Department of Shanghai Normal University and joined the 1st advanced program of Shanghai Chinese Painting Academy. He now works as a painter with Shanghai Chinese Painting Academy, and Vice-Director of its Teaching and Research Office, holding the title of Level-1 Artist. He is also a member of China Artists Association and Shanghai Artists Association.

Ma Xiaojuan

Ma Xiaojuan, born in 1955, native of Nanjing, Jiangsu Province. She obtained her master degree from the Traditional Chinese Painting Department of China Academy of Art. She works as a painter with Shanghai Chinese Painting Academy, and Director of its Teaching and Research Office, holding the title of Level-1 Artist. She is also a member of China Artists Association and Shanghai Committee of the Chinese People's Political Consultative Conference, and Director of Shanghai Artists Association and a member of its Traditional Chinese Painting Council.

Zhu Min

Zhu Min, born in 1956, native of Xinchang, Zhejiang Province, graduated from Shanghai Arts and Crafts School and the Traditional Chinese Painting Department of China Academy of Art, and joined the 1st advanced program of Shanghai Chinese Painting Academy. He works as a painter with Shanghai Chinese Painting Academy, holding the title of Level-2 Artist, and Vice Director of its Creativity and Research Office. He is also a member of Shanghai Artists Association.

Ding Xiaofang

Ding Xiaofang, born in 1957, native of Shaoxing, Zhejiang Province, graduated from the College of Fine Arts, Shanghai University and joined the 1st advanced program of Shanghai Chinese Painting Academy. He works as a painter with Shanghai Chinese Painting Academy, holding the title of Level-2 Artist, and Vice-Director of its Marketing Department. He is also a member of China Artists Association and Shanghai Artists Association.

He Xi

He Xi, born in 1960, is a native of Jiaxing, Zhejiang Province, and a graduate from the Traditional Chinese Painting Department of Zhejiang Academy of Fine Arts. He is a painter with Shanghai Chinese Painting Academy, concurrently serving as Director of the Creativity and Research Office, holding the title of Level-1 Artist. He is also a director of Shanghai Artists Association and a member of its Traditional Chinese Painting Council and China Artists Association.

译者简介

许渊冲（1921年生）

　　北京大学教授，著名翻译家，著译有中、英、法文作品百余部。中文著作有《翻译的艺术》《文学翻译谈》等；英文著作有《中诗英韵探胜——从诗经到西厢记》《逝水年华》等。英文译著有《诗经》《唐诗三百首》《西厢记》等；法文译著有《中国古诗词三百首》等。翻译过莎士比亚、德莱顿、雨果、司汤达、巴尔扎克等英法文学家的经典作品多部。

　　2010年获得中国翻译协会表彰个人的最高荣誉奖项"中国翻译文化终身成就奖"。2014年获得国际翻译界最高奖项之一——国际翻译家联盟（国际译联）2014"北极光"杰出文学翻译奖。

About the Translator

Xu Yuanchong (1921-)

Professor at Peking University, author andtranslator of over 100 literary works in Chinese, English and French. His writings in Chinese include *Art of Translation, On Literary Translation*, etc. His writings in English include *On Chinese Verse in English Rhyme: From the Book of Poetry to the Romance of the Western Bower, Vanished Springs,* etc. His English translations include *Book of Poetry*, *300 Tang Poems*, *The Romance of West Chamber*, etc. His French translations include *300 Poèmes Chinois Classiques*, etc. He has translated many classic works written by English and French literary giants such as Shakespeare, Dryden, Hugo, Stendhal and Balzac.

In 2010, Xu Yuanchong received from the Translations Association of China (TAC) "Lifetime Achievement Award", the highest honorary award for a Chinese translator. In 2014, he won the International Federation of Translators (FIT) "Aurora Borealis" Prize for Outstanding Translation of Fiction Literature, one of the highest prizes in the international translation world.

图书在版编目(CIP)数据

画说唐诗：汉英对照/许渊冲译；陈佩秋等绘.
－北京：中译出版社，2017.11（2020.6重印）
ISBN 978-7-5001-5436-5

Ⅰ.①画… Ⅱ.①许… ②陈… Ⅲ.①唐诗－诗集
－汉、英②中国画－作品集－中国－现代
Ⅳ.①I222.742②J222.7

中国版本图书馆 CIP 数据核字（2017）第 244172 号

出版发行 / 中译出版社
地　　址 / 北京市西城区车公庄大街甲 4 号物华大厦 6 层
电　　话 / (010) 68359376，68359303（发行部）68359719（编辑部）
邮　　编 / 100044
传　　真 / (010) 68357870
电子邮箱 / book@ctph.com.cn
网　　址 / http://www.ctph.com.cn

策　　划 / 许　琳　费滨海
出 品 人 / 张高里
中文审订 / 孙曼均
英文审订 / 胡晓凯
责任编辑 / 刘香玲　王　梦
装帧设计 / 吴俊青　胡小慧
印　　刷 / 山东临沂新华印刷物流集团有限责任公司

规　　格 / 787mm×1092mm　1/16
印　　张 / 23
字　　数 / 230 千字
版　　次 / 2017 年 11 月第 1 版
印　　次 / 2020 年 6 月第 8 次

ISBN 978-7-5001-5436-5　定价：98.00 元

中 译 出 版 社